Down Chick

Compilation and Introduction copyright © 2005 by Triple Crown Publications
2959 Stelzer Rd., Suite C
Columbus, Ohio 43219
www.TripleCrownPublications.com

Library of Congress Control Number: 2005929303
ISBN# 0976234947
Cover Design/Graphics: www.MarionDesigns.com
Author: Mallori McNeal
Editor: Chloé A. Hilliard
Production: Kevin J. Calloway
Consulting: Vickie M. Stringer

First Trade Paperback Edition Printing February 2005
10 9 8 7 6 5 4 3 2

Printed in the United States of America

Dedication

I dedicate this book to my grandmother Pricilla Lee. I will miss you, but I'll love you forever.

Acknowledgements

First and foremost, I want to thank God, for giving me the talent and ability to write well. Secondly, I have to thank my parents, they are the main reason for my huge imagination. To all my friends and family that read Down Chic before it was actually a novel. Thanks for the support. To Pooh, thanks for all the editing help back at SCPA, I didn't forget. To Autumn Williams, thanks for introducing me to Triple Crown, and keep writing, you could be next! To my best friends Ashley and Shavonna, Thanks for just being there. To Chris, thanks for answering all my questions. I love you and I'll always be your down chic, as long as you stay real. To Vickie Stringer, thanks for making me apart of the family, and Victoria, thank you for believing in my story. I really appreciate it. A big thanks to my editor Chloé Hilliard, thanks for pushing me to give more. To my whole entire family, I love you all, thanks for all the encouragement. Also I can't forget the readers. I can't thank you enough. To my cousin Maria, I love you and you'll always be like my sister. To my aunts Joann and Lori, thanks for the love, support and advice when I need it.

Yours Truly,

Mallori McNeal

iii

Triple Crown Publications presents

Intro

My mom named me Amina, which in Arabic means trust-worthy. "Trust is the best thing you can have in any type of relationship," is what she always told me. I grew up as an only child, which was good for me because I got a lot of attention, and good for my mom too, because she only had two mouths to feed. Her job as a secretary at a local law office was decent, so the bills were always paid and she tried her best to give me what I wanted.

Born in the Bronx, I moved to my grandmother's hometown of Cincinnati when I was ten. My mom got sick of what she called "the fast life," so we packed up and headed to the Midwest, where my grandma had moved three years before. We moved downtown to a small two-bedroom apartment on Race Street in a neighborhood called Over the Rhine. But, I spent most of my time in Avondale at my Grandmother's huge four-bedroom house. I never could figure out why my mother decided to move to downtown Cincinnati instead of just moving in with my grandmother if she was really trying to get away from the drug infested environment we were trying to escape in New York. I think the main reason she moved us all the way here was to get away from Tony, her abusive boyfriend of four years.

As I got older I didn't mind the rough streets of O.T.R. It became home and reminded me of my real home in the Bronx. The apartments were almost identical; not much to look at, but my mother and I kept our place looking and smelling clean. Sure there were pissy pew hallways and dope-fiends in every corner, but that didn't stop us from living good.

My mom was nineteen when she had me. I'm seventeen now, and all I hear is her runnin' her mouth about me keepin' my legs shut, while she out fuckin' around herself. At 36, my mother looks better than some of those hoes in the videos. I guess I can't blame her for doing her, but I just wish she would get off my back about it. I gotta do me too. I always admired my mom because she knew how to play niggas. She would have the phone ringing off the hook and wouldn't really be with any of them. I couldn't see anybody playing her because she had the game locked. I can't even say that my daddy played her, because he's the one missing out on me and her. She even played Tony from time to time, which usually caused most of the fights between them. After a while Tony got the upper hand, completely controlling my mother and her player days were over. I learned a lot from watching my mother. I always knew that when I found the right man I would be able to keep him. I would give him my loyalty, something my mother failed to give, maybe because it was never given to her.

Chapter 1

Friday - July 4, 2003

It had been a long time since me and my girls, Trina and Kelly, went out and since it was the 4th of July tonight was going to be off the hook. I met Trina and Kelly in the fifth grade at Washington Park Elementary. On my first day of school, everyone was making fun of my New York accent. Kelly, being the loud mouth, rowdy girl that she is, checked anyone that even looked at me wrong, and Trina was right next to her playing the sidekick role. After that, I became the third member of their two party clique, and we hung tight. It was rare that anyone would see us apart. Especially Kelly and me, because she lived not too far from me on 13th off of Vine Street. Trina on the other hand, lived in the suburban projects Winton Terrace. But she was with us every single day because she practically lived at Kelly's house. When high school rolled around, we all enrolled in Taft high school, downtown on Ezzard Charles. The three of us were not only the envy of the hood, but also the envy of every girl at Taft high. We had fights just about every other week and somehow managed not to get expelled. Of course the reason for the jealousy was our looks and name brand clothes that we came across so easily, thanks to the dope boys who had money and loved spending it on us.

Tonight, like many nights out on the town, we were in our head turning clothes. We rocked our hottest shit. I was always the sexiest of the clique, and I was definitely looking hot in my fitted black Lady Enyce jumper with black Manolo Timbs. Well, Steve Maddens, but I was still the shit. Both my wrists were complimented by gold bangles and around my neck was a thick herringbone and gold wire nameplate that my grandma had especially made for me on my 16th birthday. I wore the 14-karat diamond ring I had gotten from my mom, also on my 16th birthday, along with my initial and nameplate ring I had made with my own money. I loved gold and I had plenty of it. Even my nose ring was real gold. I was spoiled and that was a known fact.

We headed to the club in a black Suburban sitting on Spree wheels. It belonged to some nigga Trina was fucking around with. She was good for getting niggas whips. She kept us in something exclusive every time we went out. None of us had our own cars, but we all had licenses.

When we reached the club we stood in line for twenty minutes before flashing our fake IDs and entering. The club was thick. The D.J. was playing the hottest shit. It was like the music was hypnotizing and you couldn't help but move to the beat. All the niggas were geared up from head to toe. Some in crispy throwbacks, others in fresh white T's. There wasn't a lame nigga in sight and if there was he got his ass beat. Lames just weren't allowed. I knew I could have anybody I laid my eyes on, but at the time I just wanted to dance. So I did. I got hot; my hair was down to my shoulders and that wasn't helping any. Trying to cool off, I sat down by Kelly at the bar. As soon as I did that, she got up to dance with some dude she spotted.

"I'll be back," she said, her voice completely drowned out by the music, but it wasn't hard to read her lips. After she disappeared into the hyped crowd, I was left alone just looking around, checking out the competition, which wasn't much because as far as I was concerned I was the baddest bitch in there. Females had on everything from coochie cutters and back outs, to throw back dresses. Some fake, some real. Some even had the nerve to rock fake ass Gucci fits, and other knockoff designer shit. But that was typical for the chickens around my way.

By the end of the night, I had collected six numbers. I was satisfied. We left the club around one fifteen, which was kind of early for us. Trina wanted to leave before she got too drunk to drive home. Usually, we would have stuck around until we found some niggas to go home with.

"So, how old was those niggas you talked to?" Trina asked me on our way home.

"Two was 18, three was 19, and one 21," I told her.

"Yeah it wasn't nothing but some young boys in there tonight." She sounded like she was about 25, but in reality she was only 17, like me. I understood where she was coming from, because we all usually talked to guys over twenty. Considering that I would be 18 in November, 25 was my limit.

After Trina dropped me off at home I went straight to bed. I was drunk as hell and I knew that tomorrow I'd be suffering from a big hangover.

Triple Crown Publications presents

Chapter 2

Saturday - July 5, 2003

I didn't wake up the next day until about two o'clock in the afternoon. I dragged myself out of the bed to take a shower and get dressed. I threw on a Rocawear fit I had never worn before, with all white Air Force Ones.

It was hot as hell and everybody in the hood seemed to be out, which didn't help. I walked to 13th street, where Kelly lived. I knocked about five times before some fine ass nigga answered the door. I didn't recognize him from around the way.

"What up?" he said as if he already knew me. I didn't mind, I was planning to get to know him if Kelly wasn't already with him.

"What up, Kelly here?" I asked.

"Yeah, in the back."

As I stepped into the small apartment, the guy seemed to brush up on me. Kelly was my closest friend and she hadn't told me about a boyfriend lately except for her nigga Shawn, who I already knew but hadn't seen her with in a while. I sat down on the couch, and he went to get Kelly. About thirty seconds later, Kelly entered the living room with her cute smile.

"What up!" She sounded excited to see me.

"Shit, just seein' what was up ova dis way. You wanna go on the strip?"

"Yeah, let me grab my purse." When she came back, I got up. We were heading out the door when she said, "Oh! I didn't even introduce you. Maurice!" The guy from the door walked in the living room. "Maurice, this is my best friend Amina. Amina, this is my cousin Maurice. He stay in Mt. Auburn."

"Yeah, we kind of met at the door." He just stared at me for a second not saying anything.

"Ok, well we leavin' so I see you lata on. You still goin' to get some weed?" she asked Maurice.

"Yeah. You smoke?" he asked looking at me again.

"Yeah." I glanced at the small scar on the right side of his face. It was somewhat attractive.

"Come back through then."

"Aight."

Kelly and I caught a bus to the strip in Clifton and of course it was thick with niggas, just the way we liked it. I picked up a few clothes from Lady Exclusive while we were there. When I got back to my apartment, I was tired. I took a two hour nap. As soon as I woke up I called Kelly. She suggested I just stay the night with her. I agreed because I knew I wouldn't feel like walking back home late at night.

First, I got permission from my mom, who of course approved. Then, I packed some clothes into my overnight bag, grabbed some more money out of my stash and left.

When I got to Kelly's she was laid up on the couch with Shawn. Maurice was on the other couch rolling a joint.

"Come on, we got that shit ova here," she laughed.

"What up Mina?" Shawn said.

"What up, where you been at?" I asked, curious about why I hadn't seen him in a while. Kelly and him were usually inseparable. He was an all around thug, but he treated her good.

"Makin' runs and shit. You know how it is," he replied.

"Yeah." I knew exactly what he meant. Shawn was one of the big time dope boys around our way, unlike some of the younger ones who really didn't know shit. He was five years older than us, which was Kelly's limit.

I walked into Kelly's room to put down my bags. As soon I turned around, she was in my face. "Hey, I was thinkin' you could chill with Maurice tonight, after we smoke and shit. It's been a while for me and Shawn, so you know what I'm tryna do." She was whispering like it was a crime for her to ask me.

"Yeah, that's cool." I told her. I could understand that they needed some time alone. Besides, I was kind of happy about having somebody to be with for the night. It had been a while for me too, at least a month.

"Ok, we ain't leavin' but you can have my room, and I'll take Sandra's room She don't get off 'till tomorrow morning." Sandra was Kelly's mom. She always called her by her first name because they never really got along.

"Aight, but I don't know if we takin' it to the bed," I lied. I wanted some pipe bad, and I had a feeling I would get it tonight.

"Bitch please. After a few hits of that dro and some Hen. you gon' be gettin fucked whether you want to or not."

"Who got Henessy?"

"Shawn brought it. He brought some Grey Goose and Tang too cause I don't really fuck with Hen no more."

"Well, I guess I really ain't got no choice huh?" I laughed.

"Nope," she said, leading the way back into the living room where Maurice and Shawn had already started smoking. She took the joint from Shawn, hitting it three times to the face. That's how we always did it. I sat next to Maurice, and after hitting the dro about four times he started looking even sexier. I had four more hits and some Tangeray before I was through. Kelly and Shawn went to Sandra's room leaving me and Maurice alone, staring at each other high as fuck.

"Come on." He took my hand leading me back to Kelly's room. He sat on the bed and grabbed my hands pulling me closer to him. We kissed and the next thing I knew I had straddled him in a riding position and went full speed. It hurt but I kept going, I had no mercy on myself. I was moaning, and it seemed to excite him, I could feel his dick getting harder inside of me. He held my hips as I moved back and forth. After I came, we switched positions and he got on top of me. As soon as he entered he began pounding at my pussy making me cum three times in a row before he did. When he was finished he got right up.

"Damn, yo shit was wet," he said zipping up his pants.

"I know." He left the room and went outside, somewhere down the block. I just wanted to go to sleep. I took a shower, laid down on the living room couch and ended up falling asleep.

Most people would consider what I did a hoe move. I won't even blame it on the weed or drink, because I would have done it either way. To me it was just a horny move. I needed it and why turn it down if it was right there in my face?

Chapter 3

Sunday - July 6, 2003

When I got home Sunday afternoon, I checked the mailbox. I knew my mom was good for forgetting to check the mail, and sure enough I was right, there was still mail from Saturday— three bills for my mom, an Essence magazine, and a letter addressed to me from Damen Costello. For a minute the name drew a blank in my head. Then I realized...it was my father. I looked at the return address, it was local. Was he living in Cincinnati?

Dear Amina,

How have you been? Good, I hope. I know you've never met me, but I would really like it to happen one day. I feel like I missed out on you, and I just want to make up for the lost time. I don't know how to explain my absence, so I won't even try. I hope you will find it in your heart to forgive me and give me a shot at being your father. I know this may all be a big shock to you, and I understand. I won't rush you; take as much time as you need to think about it. Give me a call when you are ready if you decide that's what you want to do. My number is (513) 555-6896.

P.S. I have a surprise for you!

Love Always,

Damen Costello

By the time I reached the end of the letter, hot tears had gathered in my eyes and ran down my face. These were not tears of happiness, but at the same time they weren't exactly tears of pain. These tears represented a strong feeling of confusion and anger mixed together. I was so confused about what would make him want to come into my life after all these years. I was angry that it took so long for me to hear from him.

In an instant, I had made up my mind. I would meet him, but I sure wasn't about to make it real easy on his ass. This definitely wasn't going to be the long-lost daughter, happy reunion type situation played out on TV. Shit, I was far from long-lost. The real question is; where was he? Probably doing who knows what, missing out on his smart and beautiful daughter who doesn't need him anyway.

While these thoughts ran through my head, I wondered what my mom would think. A couple of hours later, I was awoken from my nap when I heard her come in.

"Hey," she said cheerfully, appearing in my doorway.

"Hi," I replied solemnly.

"What's wrong?"

"Nothing, just woke up."

"I think I'm 'bout to take a lil' nap myself. You have fun last night, drunky?" she laughed.

"Yeah," I answered. I didn't have to try to play dumb with her; she already knew everything I did. There was nothing to hide.

"What's that?" she asked, looking at the letter. I had fallen asleep with it in my hand.

"A letter."

"From who?"

"Damen."

"Who?"

"Damen Costello."

Her whole mood changed. She looked shocked. She took the letter and read it. "Angie told me she saw him when she was in Brooklyn visiting a friend, she probably gave him the address." Angie was my mom's older sister and my favorite aunt. She lived in Baltimore. "Have you thought about it?" she asked when she was done.

"Yeah, I'm gonna meet him," I sighed.

"Ok, you sure about this, you don't have to. You know you don't owe him anything." She sounded like she didn't want me to do it.

"I know, Ma. I just want to."

"Ok, baby." She kissed me on my forehead and left my room. I fell asleep again, and woke up about two hours later to a completely dark room. It was storming and flashes of lightning lit up my room. I got up to close my blinds, and open my door to let some air in. The apartment was completely silent, with the exception of the thunder going on outside. I figured my mom was still sleep or had gone out, but I didn't bother to look. Instead, I got right back in my bed. I didn't feel like moving, talking, or even looking at anybody.

I had a funny feeling in my stomach. I tried to keep my mind clear and off the letter. But less than two minutes later, I found myself thinking about it again. My mind was reviewing everything the letter said. I wondered what the surprise was. What could a man that I had never met, have for me? What made him think he could give me a surprise? How did he even know what I liked? Questions, questions, and more questions that I couldn't answer for myself piled up inside my head. I decided to put my frustration to rest again. I closed my eyes and went back to sleep.

Chapter 4

Saturday - July 12, 2003

Another night spent home alone. A week had passed since I got the letter, and I still hadn't gotten up the nerve to call. I decided now was the time. I dialed the number and a deep voice answered on the second ring.

"Hello?"

"Is this Damen?" I asked in a calm voice.

"Yes, who is this?"

"Amina."

"Oh, I see you took up my offer."

"Something like that," I said cold as hell.

"Ok. You're probably wondering how I got your address. I saw your Aunt Angie a few weeks ago. She gave it to me."

"Why didn't you just get the house number?"

"I thought writing you would be better, I didn't want to scare you away. I just wanted to let you think about it and call if you wanted to."

"So, if I hadn't called would you have been mad?"

"Well, I don't think I would be mad, a little disappointed though. I couldn't blame you though."

"So, when are we supposed to meet?"

"It's all up to you. I'm working with your schedule."

I liked the way he seemed to be kissing my ass so I had a little fun. "Well, I'm busy all this week, so is next Saturday the 19th good?"

"Yeah, that's perfect." He sounded excited.

"You know what? I'm sorry I am busy Saturday. Let's make it Sunday," I lied.

"Even better. What time?"

"Two is good."

"It's a date then."

"You know how to get here right?"

"Yeah, I'll find it ok."

"Alright. I'll see you then."

"Ok."

We hung up, and my mom came in immediately afterwards.

"I just talked to Damen," I told her.

"What'd he say?"

"He's going to come over next Sunday."

"Alright." She seemed unfazed by the news. "I'm going out for a while. There's money on the table. You can order a pizza if you get hungry."

"OK." That's exactly what I did after she left. I ate a whole large pepperoni pizza by myself, and didn't think twice about it.

Sunday – July 20, 2003

The week went by in a flash and before I knew it, it was time to meet Damen. I woke up unusually early, around 10 o'clock. My normal wake up time in the summer was noon. I guess I was just excited. I didn't sleep well at all the night before. But when I got up I didn't feel sleepy. I lounged around on the couch until 12:45. Then I took a shower and decided on a comfortable jean dress by Pepe. I wore my fresh white K-Swiss. I pulled my hair into a low side ponytail. After adding my jewelry I was complete. By now it was 1:40 p.m. An hour had passed that quickly.

"You look pretty," my mom said, as she walked up behind me in the mirror.

"Thanks. You do too." She was wearing a soft cream colored dress, casual but sexy; it fit her in all the right places. I wondered if she was trying to impress Damen, or maybe just giving him a peek of what he was missing out on.

"I'm gonna go get the food ready." She went to the kitchen to take out the pasta salad she made and fresh breadsticks baking in the oven. The smell of them got my appetite up. I sat in my room until I heard a loud knock at the door at exactly two p.m.

I can't believe he's on time, I thought to myself. My mom appeared in my doorway.

"You want to get it?" she asked grinning.

"No, you get it," I said nervously. She disappeared, leaving me sitting in my room. I heard the door slowly open.

"Hi, Kayla." Damen handed my mother a large bouquet of flowers.

"Hello Damen. Long time no see." She looked down at the flowers, unimpressed.

"I know, I'm here to make up for that time."

"Good luck," she said reaching for the flowers. "Amina!" I took a deep breath and walked into the living room.

"Is this Amina? She's beautiful," he said in awe. I looked him up and down without saying a word. He was tall, with light brown eyes, honey glazed skin and wore his hair low with a well cut goatee. My daddy was fine. His smile displayed his perfectly white teeth and deep dimples. He wore a red silk shirt and black slacks with black gators. His scent was pleasant. I didn't recognize the cologne, but it smelled expensive. Probably not as expensive as that watch on his wrist though.

Nervously, I smiled back. "Hi," I finally replied. We hugged then sat down on the couch. After five minutes of discussion his cell phone rang, interrupting me in mid-sentence.

"Your surprise is on the way," he said after finishing his brief phone conversation.

"What is it?" I asked as if I believed he was going to ruin it by telling me. He looked at my mother; they both cracked a sneaky smile. "Ma, you know?"

"Yeah. I called him last week to make sure it was something you would like."

"Will I like it?" I asked anxiously.

"I don't know," she answered. This really confused me.

"I hope so," Damen chimed in.

We sat in silence for five minutes and there was a knock at the door. My mom opened it and a tall brown skin guy stepped in. He hugged my mother respectfully and greeted Damen with a "what's up?" I was definitely confused now. I knew this wasn't some type of match-maker shit they had going on. But if it was I wouldn't have complained because he was sexy. He stood almost as tall as my father, with the same color skin and eyes as him. He had 360 waves and was rocking Sean John from head to toe. Of course Air Force Ones were on his feet, and I couldn't help but notice the chain hanging around his neck. The cross held real diamonds, not rhinestones. His watch was just as impressive. He looked at me and smiled, but not in a seductive way, which threw me off. He seemed to already know me. I know I didn't know him...at all. I did recognize how pretty his smile was though, with his perfect teeth, and deep dimples. I put two and two together and realized he was my brother.

"Amina, this is your brother Azelle," Damen said.

"What up?" Azelle said so casual you would think he knew me all his life.

"Hi," I said giving him an uncertain look.

We all sat down to eat, but my appetite was gone after I found out that Damen and Azelle's mom were married up until 2001. They used to live in Chicago until after their divorce. Then Damen and Azelle moved to Cincinnati. Azelle, 23, had an apartment in Corryville, and Damen had a house in Indian Hills. I couldn't understand why Azelle, aka Zelle, had Damen around since day one and my day one was just now swinging around. I didn't bother to ask because no excuse in the world would have been good enough for me.

We talked for hours. It was mostly my mom telling every little story from my childhood she could think of. She completely ran off at the mouth. She even pulled out baby pictures. But I wasn't embarrassed because I was a pretty little girl. I was surprised at how excited she seemed to be. We never went into what happened between him and my mother, but he did tell me that he looked for us for years but he didn't know that we moved to Cincinnati, which was where he was originally from. I felt more at ease knowing that he at least tried to find me, and for the rest of his visit I was more open and much more pleasant. I felt he deserved a little credit rather than none.

When Damen and Azelle left I was ready to sleep again. I

was glad I had the chance to meet Damen, and I was even happier to have an older brother to get to know.

Chapter 5

Saturday - July 26, 2003

It seemed like everybody was at the movies. As soon as Azelle and I walked in, I saw, Brell and Swag, two of my niggas that lived close to me. Like Kelly and Trina, I had known them since fifth grade and they were always like brothers to me. Any problems I had, I would run to them and they would handle it. I introduced them to Azelle before they went to their movie. Azelle went all out, buying popcorn, nachos, candy and ice cream. We spent so much time at the concession stand that we barely made the beginning of the movie. Honestly, I was glad, I hate watching the previews.

When the movie was over, I noticed even more people were there. In the lobby, the police had started kicking people out who they assumed were about to start trouble. That's how it always was in the hood. Whenever too many niggas were in one place at a time, they were quickly moved out. The police obviously hadn't made it outside to the parking lot yet, because it was like a club out there. Niggas were sitting in their cars just stuntin', letting their spinners spin. Females were breaking their necks trying to be the first to get a holla from the niggas who had the cars. All eyes were on me and Azelle when we got in his all black Escalade with lush tan leather seats and spinners that never stopped.

I noticed a girl named Amber that I knew. She lived in Covington, Kentucky, but she was always in my hood with some lame nigga named Freddy. I never cared for her. She was sitting on the hood of an old school with her sidekick, some girl I never knew but had always seen her with. They went well together. They were both brown skinned; cute, but not really sexy. They were both skinny with no kind of ass or titties to make the revealing clothes they wore even worth putting on and both had their eyes glued to Zelle.

"I'ma get him," Amber announced loud enough for me to hear. Azelle didn't notice her. He was busy changing the channel on his front seat TV. I gave her a challenging look. I couldn't wait for her to try to talk to my brother. I would have something for that ass.

"You hungry?" Azelle asked me as we pulled out of the parking lot.

"Yeah, what we eatin'?"

"It's up to you."

"Aight." I suggested a burger place that was close. At the restaurant I looked over the limited menu and finally decided on a specialty burger and steak fries.

"I'll have the same," Azelle told the waitress after me.

"Alright. I'll take your menus," she said flipping her long blonde hair, and walking away switching her hips so hard they looked like they would fall off. She was in desperate need of a few make-up tips because her black eyeliner was way too dark for her pale skin. She looked like a cracked out raccoon. When she showed up again with our food and drinks, we both tried to hold our laughs in but it didn't work. She gave us a funny look and switched away.

"How much was your car?" I asked Azelle starting up a conversation.

"Damen gave it to me. I worked for him for two years at the dealership back in Chicago before we moved here. That car is about four years old, but I hooked it up this year with new TV's and my authentic rims. When I first got 'em, people hadn't never seen no shit like that before. I had people blowin' horns and tellin' me something was wrong with my rims, 'cause they never stop spinnin'. Ain't that crazy?"

"Yeah, that's crazy as hell. You call him by his first name?"

"Yeah, we tight like that. He don't like me callin' him dad. He say it make 'em feel old. He the type of nigga that don't ever wanna get old," he smiled.

"Yeah, that's how my mom is too, but we definitely have our times. It ain't always cool between us, she can be controlling when she wants to," I chuckled. I wish me and my mom was as tight as Azelle and Damen. They seemed to be more friends than father and son.

"That's how mom's are, especially with girls, she just lookin' out for you. It would be ignorant for her not to," he laughed.

"So you miss your mom?"

"Yeah. I even missed her when I moved out the house in Chicago and got my own crib there. I love my momma. I go back every time I get a chance."

"Oh, so you a momma's boy, huh?"

"Don't tell nobody," he grinned.

"What made you move here?"

"I just decided to move here with Damen after my parents divorced. I was always used to being around him so it made sense to come with him, and my mom didn't mind, she knew we were close.

"Did Damen ever say anything to you about me?"

"When I was seventeen, he mentioned that I had a sister somewhere. He never involved me in his search for you, but I do remember him going to the Bronx at least twice and coming back with nothing. I think after a while he kind of gave up. Then about three weeks ago we was in Brooklyn visiting one of his old friends and he ran into your aunt and she gave him the address. He was excited, but I could tell he was nervous as hell 'cause the rest of the trip he was quiet and stayed to himself like he was thinkin' real hard. I asked him if he wanted me to write you 'cause I thought maybe you would be more relaxed with me, but he wanted to do it. He said it was something he had to do. I'm just glad you ain't bust his nuts 'cause he probably would've never got over it."

"Yeah," I agreed. We both fell quiet as we continued to eat.

"You seventeen, right?" he asked breaking the silence, looking at me like he had an idea.

"Yup," I answered.

"Damen will probably take you to the dealership he just opened in Springdale and let you pick out a car."

"You think so?" I asked with excitement.

"Yeah. I got my first car by working for him. I didn't have to because he had already offered me one. But me bein' me, I wanted to earn it."

"I can drive, but my mom doesn't want me driving her car. I don't know why though. Maybe because she just got it. She love that lil' Honda."

"You ain't gotta worry 'bout that with Damen. He gon' spoil you."

"I'd love that." I thought about what he said about wanting to earn his first car. I liked that idea. But I also liked the idea of having an option of working for it or not. "Maybe I'll work for it like you did," I said.

"That's the best way," he smiled. Already I loved Azelle. I liked the way he talked to me, and I had a feeling he would protect me.

When we finished our food he got up to pay the check. He stopped back at the table to leave the waitress a tip. He laid down a $5 bill and looked at me.

"Na, her nasty lookin' ass get two dollas." We both laughed and he took the five back replacing it with two singles.

"Thanks for the food and movie," I said, grateful that I didn't have to break my last fifty.

"You my lil' sister whatever you want, you got."

"Ok." It felt so good to have someone to look out for me. On the ride home, we cracked jokes and he told me what my father was like when he was growing up. I realized that all three of us had a lot in common—we were all stubborn and hot-tempered.

"You got a lil' boyfriend?" he asked like I wasn't supposed to.

"No," I answered quickly. I could tell by the way he asked that he was overprotective.

"Keep it like that 'till you about thirty."

I laughed but the look on his face was serious. "Yeah, ok Azelle whatever."

"Call me Zelle."

"Ok *Zelle*," I corrected myself. He pulled up in front of my apartment building, and looked at his iced out watch.

"It's 11:30. Past your bedtime," he laughed, getting out of the car.

"Yeah right, Amina Li'Auna Moore, don't have no bedtime."

He opened my door and walked me up the steps. "Well,

Amina Li'Auna Costello do." He could tell I was thinking about what he just said. "What? You don't like me to call you by our last name?"

"Na. It's kind of cute. Just ain't used to it, that's all."

"My bad. I was just playin' with you."

"Oh, it's cool. So how did we end up with a name like Costello anyway?" I asked as he walked me to my building.

"Our great granddaddy was Latino."

"For real? So that's where I get my good hair from?" I laughed.

"Yeah, maybe," "You can't really tell though. I don't see it in Damen. I guess he took after grandma, she was brown-skinned."

"You knew her?" I leaned up against the banister.

"Yeah, she died three years ago of a heart attack. And Granddaddy was killed before I was born."

"By who?"

"I don't know, he was in some Brooklyn mafia back in the day."

"Why did Damen move to Chicago if he was born here?"

"Granddaddy was from Brooklyn, but grandma was from here. They got divorced because she got sick of him running back and forth to New York with the little mafia he was in. When they divorced he moved back to New York, Damen and his brother Roscoe moved with him. He met my mom there, they had me real young. We lived there until I was four then my mom got accepted to the University of Chicago, so we left. I already told you how we ended up here."

"What were our grandparents' names?"

"Cassandra and Angelo."

"Where did Cassandra live in Cincinnati."

"She had a house out in Price Hill. After she died Damen sold it."

"Oh," I replied ending my interrogation.

"So, you good on the family history now?" he smiled.

"Yeah."

"I can't blame you. I would wanna know some stuff about my peoples too if I had never met 'em." Silently, I looked down at the floor. "What's wrong?" he asked looking down at me, trying to find my eyes.

"Nothin' I'm good." I looked up.

"A, I'll pick you up next Saturday and take you to see my place and the dealership. Maybe you can pick out that car." He was trying to cheer me up. It worked. I couldn't help but cracked a smile as I unlocked the front door.

"I won't come in, it's late. Tell your mom I said hi, aight?"

"I will."

"Be safe." He gave me a hug and left.

When I got inside, my apartment was dark; the kitchen light was the only one on. I threw my purse down on the living room couch, and walked over to the kitchen table to pick up the note I saw.

Mina –

I'm out with a friend from work. I should be back by 1 a.m. at the latest.

Love,

Mommy

I looked at my watch; it was 11:38. I wondered who her "friend" was. I was hoping she was out with a rich lawyer from her office, and that they would become more than friends. I undressed and got in bed. All of a sudden, I felt sleepy which was strange. It was still early, and I had slept in late today. But that didn't stop me from falling asleep as soon as my head hit the pillow.

Chapter 6

Saturday - August 2, 2003

I woke up at seven o'clock in the morning. My mouth was watering. I stumbled out of the bed and ran down the hall to the bathroom just in time for my vomit to make it in the toilet. After throwing up for about a minute straight, I sat down on the bathroom floor. My head was spinning like a Ferris Wheel, but faster. Before I get it together, my mom walked in.

"You sick?" she asked eyes half-closed.

"Yeah, it must have been something I ate," I lied. I knew it wasn't that. My period was a week and a half late. I had to be pregnant.

"You want some Mylanta? It'll help settle your stomach."

"Yeah." I dreaded having to swallow that nasty shit. But I did it just to make my sickness seem normal. Then I went into the kitchen for a glass of water. After washing down the lumps in my throat, I went back to bed. I was relieved my mom didn't ask me about being pregnant. But I knew if this didn't pass, the question would pop up real soon.

I got up again at two o'clock to get ready for Zelle, who was picking me up to go to Damen's dealership.

"Damen here?" he asked the secretary at the front desk of the dealership, next to where the display cars were kept.

"Yeah, in his office," she smiled in a flirtatious way. She looked like one of those scandalous hoes. She thought she was a dime. She had a long ponytail, or shall I say long horsehair, because, that's what it was. She was a caramel complexion with green eyes. Anybody could tell they were contacts. Her shirt was so low, her titties damn near popped out. She was trying so hard to look good, but she still didn't have shit on me. The moment she looked at me and gave me a phony smile was the same moment I became determined to take her place at that desk, leaving her without a job.

When we got in Damen's office he was on the phone. I didn't pay attention to his conversation, I was busy looking around. He had two framed 22-inch rims along with countless other awards that hung on his back wall. The rims were an award for selling the best rims in Chicago. Another plaque was signed by the mayor of Chicago for being the *1st place Cadillac dealer in the city of Chicago*. It was awarded to Costello's Cadillac Dealership and Car Essentials. Pictures of him and Zelle were all around the office. He also had group pictures of him and all of his male workers. One from the dealership he had owned in Chicago and the other one with his staff in Brooklyn. It was about 15 workers in each picture and they all looked about Zelle's age. Some maybe were older, but they all were either cute or sexy.

"Hey princess," Damen greeted me with a smile, as soon as he got off the phone.

"Hi," I said in a sweet tone.

"I see your big brother decided to bring you up to see my money making headquarters."

"Yup," I answered. Money making headquarters was exactly what this place was. I knew that just by looking at the expensive furniture in the office. There was a silver chrome desk with a matching chair, a flat screen TV and two huge cream leather love seats positioned in the two corners across from his desk. I sat in one; Zelle in the other.

"I'ma take her to my apartment when we leave," Zelle chimed in.

"Ok. Come on, I'll show you around." Damen got up to lead me outside. He stopped by the girl at the front desk. "Did Shayna call?" he asked her. She was filing her fingernails, and indulging in a phone conversation. Her facial expression made it obvious she wasn't on a business call.

"No." She looked at Damen, licking her lips as if she wanted to fuck him right there in front of me. He didn't even give her the attention she seemed so desperate for. Instead he turned to me, smiling proudly.

"Camele, this is my daughter Amina. Amina, this is Camele my secretary, Amina is seventeen she'll probably be working for me soon. Ain't that right princess?"

"Yeah." I threw the phony smile she had given me earlier back in her face. She gave me a cold hard stare before choking up a simple "Hi."

"Hi," I replied back before I walked away with Damen.

There were at least fifty Cadillacs on the lot, ranging from cars to SUV's. He even had about ten old school Caddy's for sale. As we walked through the lot, I couldn't help but picture myself behind the wheel of every car I spotted. But there was an Escalade EXT that caught my eye immediately. It was painted a pretty royal blue, my color, and parked near the front of the lot. I admired the trucks color as the sun beamed on its new paint.

"Those are the cars I don't really sell too much of." He pointed to the old school Caddys . "But don't get me wrong, they do sell. I try to accentuate everyone's style. Most dealers don't sell old school but I do," he explained. I was still staring at the blue truck.

"You seem like a really good salesmen," I commented as we walked to the spacious garage off to the side.

"Well, I try to do my best," he laughed.

There were all types of rims displayed on the left wall. There was a big poster of different color paints for cars. Towards the back was a big glass display case with TV's and sound systems inside. Beside it was a magazine rack holding car accessory magazines.

"These are all of my car accessories. You know you gotta have the whole package. So, when you buy a car you can come and get it hooked up in here. Or even if you don't buy a car you can still get car accessories here. There are a lot of options on display but there are even more in the magazines we have." I looked around amazed at all the things that could be put into one car. "We also do design leather seating, personalized head rests, dashboards and so on."

"Oh ok, so your customers get everything in one place."

"Yup, and I've been getting business since the day I opened."

"When did you open?"

"I opened up in April, but everything wasn't fully put together until June."

"I heard about it a few times on the radio, but for some reason the name didn't click in my head. I even know people who have bought cars from here."

"It shouldn't have had to click in your head, I should have been there from the start, but I just wasn't ready to step up. I knew I had a wife and kid already, and I thought if I brought you in the picture it would mess everything up. I was wrong for that. I should have taken responsibility for what I did."

"So I was just a mistake?"

"To be honest, that's what I would have called it then, but looking at you now I can't call you a mistake. Obviously you were meant to be born."

"Did my mom know you were married?"

"Yeah, she knew. I married Zelle's mom at twenty, and of course I knew nothing about being a husband. We were together three years before we decided getting married was the right thing to do. I was seventeen when Zelle was born and she was fourteen, so we weren't really ready to settle down. She did her thing for a while and so did I. I guess I just never stopped even after we were married."

"How did you and my mom meet?"

"She was living in Brooklyn with your Aunt Angie. I'm sure you already know that but anyway, I was still living in Brooklyn a few years after my father was killed. I met your mom at my brother's 25th birthday party that your Aunt Angie threw him. They were together at the time."

"So when did I come in?" I wanted him to hurry up and get to the good part—me.

"Well, me and your mom were messing around for a few months. A month after I left for Chicago, I got the news that my brother, Roscoe, had been shot, and then came the news that your mom was pregnant with you. I fell under the pressure, and the only thing I knew to do was run from my problems. After his funeral I never went back to New York."

"Do you know who shot him?"

"Police never found out, I tortured about fifteen niggas from Brooklyn and nobody knew who did it or they just wasn't trying to tell. I would have killed whoever shot him. My brother was my life; he was just like my father. I looked up to him, so it hit me real hard when he was killed. I wish he was still living so you could meet him."

"Is that when Aunt Angie moved to Baltimore."

"Yeah. Her and Roscoe were tight. They had been together for five years. But I guess she just needed to get away. So she did, and that's when your mom moved to the Bronx."

"How did you know?"

"Well, we talked at the funeral for the last time. Angie had already made up her mind that she wanted out of Brooklyn, so your mom went to the Bronx with your grandmother."

"Oh," I replied. I had no more questions on the subject; I already knew that part of the story.

"You know, I don't know how many times I can tell you this without you getting sick of hearing it, but I'm sorry. And I really do love you, believe it or not."

"Yeah, I guess a part of me loves you for coming back around and being honest." He looked at me without saying anything. The look in his eyes was as if he was moved by my comment. "So is the dealership closed today?" I changed the subject to lighten the mood.

"No, just the garage. It's always closed the last work day of the month for inventory. The dealership is always closed on Sundays."

"Oh, is Camele good help?" I asked anxious to hear how he felt about her.

"Yeah, she's good. A real trip sometimes, but she gets the job done."

"And the rest of your workers only work in the garage?"

"Yeah, that's my garage crew, they work really hard; we stay busy. It's just me and Camele in the office on days like these."

"I see." We walked back inside. Zelle was knocked out sleep on Damen's loveseat.

"Wake up. Your sister is ready to go," he smacked him in the head laughing. They seemed more like niggas than father and son. Zelle looked at me as if I was from another planet when he opened his eyes. I laughed and then sat down on the arm of the chair.

"Come on," I said.

"Aight. Let's go." He got out of the chair.

I gave Damen a hug and we left.

Zelle lived on the right side of a nice two family house on Eden Street. The apartment had shiny hard wood floors, a huge flat screen that was mounted directly across from the walnut colored leather couch with matching love seats. The area rug was a cream color and the walls were painted a honey brown, which tied all the neutrals together. His DVD and CD collection were arranged across the top of the wall like a boarder, in a snake shaped CD shelf. There were at least 150 CD's there. There were speakers in all four corners of the living room that served as the surround sound to his entertainment center.

"Damn," was all I could say. We walked past his wood decorated kitchen and breakfast bar that substituted as a kitchen table to his bedroom. It was spacious and decorated in all black and white—black comforter, black furniture and a black and white checkered rug. Another flat screen and DVD player sat in his main wall. He had a bathroom off to the side. It was decorated in black and white marble, and cleaner than any nigga's bathroom I had ever seen. In his walk-in closet, all his clothes were color coordinated. His shoes were lined neatly across the floor. There were about 50 pairs. All of them were either Air Force Ones or Jordans.

"You hire an interior decorator in here?"

"Na, this broad I used to fuck with did all this. She was big on decoratin' and shit like that."

"How long were you together?"

"I was never with her. She was just on a paper chase. I knew it from the start. I just let her have some fun, made her think she was special. I took her on one or two shoppin' sprees, told her to hook my shit up and she thought we was in love. That's when I cut her ass off; I ain't got time for all that shit."

"Oh, I feel you." I sat on his bed, still amazed by his neatness and good taste.

"Amina, don't ever fuck with no nigga like me, we ain't no good."

"What you mean like you?"

"A dope boy, we don't have time for love, we don't even wanna make time. Remember that." Little did he know that all I ever messed with was dope boys. It was a wonder I hadn't accidentally started talking to him considering the money he had. He led me to an empty room next to his, and began a new conversation before I had a chance to respond to his warning.

"You can do whatever you want with this room."

"This me?" I asked with a huge Kool Aid smile on my face.

"Yeah, I ain't doin' shit with it, might as well be yours for when you come stay with me."

"Thanks." I liked the room. It was a little smaller than his, with a walk-in closet, but no bathroom.

"And you can use the bathroom across the hall. I don't use it but my niggas do when they come over."

"That's fine, I don't mind." The bathroom wasn't as spacious as his but it was clean with a white marble sink.

"I'll take you to get whatever you need to fix up this room. If you wanna paint that's cool too, just let me know."

"Ok, I probably will. But I'll let you know when I figure out what I wanna do with it."

"Aight. You hungry? Want somethin' to eat?"

"Yeah."

"Ain't shit in the crib, but we can go get somethin.' You like Uno's?"

"Yeah."

"You wanna go there?"

"Yeah, that sounds good."

We headed over to Uno's on Ludlow. After we ordered our food, it hit me; maybe I should tell Zelle about my morning sickness. I needed to tell somebody, but I wasn't ready to tell my mom yet.

"Zelle?" I whispered.

"What's up?"

I was silent for a minute because I didn't know what to say or how to say it. I wanted to ask him to take me to get a pregnancy test, but I didn't want him to look at me any different. "Nevermind," I said nonchalantly.

"Na, go head. What's on yo mind?" He sounded concerned.

"Nothin'," I said as the waitress sat down our food interrupting our conversation. We both took a slice of pizza and began eating.

"What you wanna ask me Mina?" He had never called me that before. It surprised me.

"It wasn't really a question," I mumbled.

"What, you pregnant or somethin'?" The question came out of nowhere, but it sounded a lot better coming from him than it would have coming from my mom. I looked down at my plate and started picking the crust off my pizza.

"You gon' answer my question?" he pressed.

I looked up at him. "I don't know. I was throwin' up this mornin' plus I missed my shit last month." I purposely left out the word "period." It would have spoiled my appetite, so I'm sure it would have spoiled his.

He turned his head towards the window, looking disappointed. "Who you fuck, I thought you said you ain't have a nigga."

"I don't, it was somebody I met."

"Oh, just some random nigga, huh?"

"Somethin' like that." I could have smacked my self for saying that, because the look he gave me was foul. If looks could kill I would have been dead on the spot.

"So who is he?" he continued.

"My best friend's cousin. His name is Maurice, he's from Mt. Auburn."

"Where he stay at out there?"

"I don't know what street."

"Damn. You don't know shit bout this nigga and you got 'em, right?"

"I was high, and I had been drinkin'."

"What type of shit is that? You better than that."

"I know. I just fucked up."

"What's his name again?"

"Maurice."

"Short dude, brown skin, gotta scar on the right side of his face?"

"Yeah, you know him?" I answered, remembering the scar on his cheek that I thought was so sexy.

"Yeah. I know him." He rolled his eyes, as if to say he couldn't stand him. But I didn't ask anymore questions. "Excuse me," he said catching the attention of the waitress who was on her way to another table with drinks. "Can we have some boxes for this stuff, and the check too?"

"Sure," she said real sincere. She was just gaming to get a good tip. I looked at him confused. No more than a minute later she was back with what he requested. He packed the food into the boxes. I didn't care because I had lost my appetite after that look he gave me. He put down the exact amount for the check and left a five dollar tip.

"Let's go." His tone made it clear to me that he was heated. If I would have known he was going to react that way, I never would have told him. We drove over to the strip and he pulled in the Wallgreen's parking lot.

"What up nigga?" I heard a voice say. I looked up and saw a tall sexy redbone with a neatly trimmed goatee and waves that made me sea sick, standing in front of a maroon Yukon. His car door was open displaying his Louis Vuitton seats, and dashboard TV.

"What up?" Zelle replied, giving him the normal nigga handshake.

"This you?" He looked at me.

"Na, my lil' sister."

"Oh foreal? What's up Shorty? My name Kayne," he introduced himself, holding his hand out for a handshake. I shook it and smiled at him. He was another new face and a beautiful one at that.

"I'm Amina," I said. I could feel Zelle staring the whole time. Another nigga came across the street and joined the conversation between Kayne and Zelle. I didn't really pay any attention to his appearance. I was busy scoping Kayne out in his fresh Akademiks fit and icy white Air Force Ones. The medallion around his neck was a huge diamond studded K and shined like Zelle's, almost blinding my eyes. He also had on a blinding Cartier watch.

"Here." Zelle handed me a fifty. "You know what you need to get," he said nodding towards Wallgreen's. Nervously, I went into the store and walked up and down each isle. I was surprised when Kayne snuck up behind me while I was debating on which test to get.

"We ain't really get a chance to talk outside, I wanted to get at you but I wasn't tryin' to see Zelle sweatin' me and shit. So what's up?" He gave me a sexy grin, displaying his perfectly white teeth.

"You tell me," I said, walking away from the pregnancy test area.

"You gon' let me call you?" I recited my number and he put it in his Nextel walkie-talkie that had been chirping since he walked in the store. "Where you goin? I thought you came in here to get something." He gave me another grin as if he knew something I didn't.

"Oh yeah, I did." I played it off leaving him and walking back towards the tests. I picked two that I thought I could trust and walked back to the counter. I figured he would've been gone but he stood there by the counter waiting on me. The cashier rang the test up, looking back and forth at me and Kayne. She must have thought he was the father of my possible baby. Kayne laughed at her misconception, but I didn't.

When we got back outside Zelle was still talking to the other nigga that had walked up on the scene. "You ready?" He eyed Kayne suspiciously, who was standing next to me. Kayne paid it no mind.

"Yeah," I said, but what I really meant was no. I wanted to

stay and talk with Kayne. I knew Zelle wasn't with it though. So I followed him back to the car.

"Take yo lil' fast ass in the bathroom and do what you gotta do," he said as soon as we got inside. I headed to my bathroom, and quickly closed the door. I took a deep breath then opened the first test. It took about two minutes for me to go to the bathroom. It felt like it took even longer for the response—the positive symbol appeared. I broke down in tears. I tried not to be too loud, so that Zelle wouldn't hear. I pulled myself together just long enough to try the second test. It was no help because it showed a positive sign too. I was pregnant for sure, and there was no way around it. I looked in the mirror and my reflection scared me. My eyes had turned puffy from crying, and my skin looked dried out. As I stared into my own eyes the room started spinning. I attempted to turn and open the bathroom door, but before I could even leave out, my stomach forced up the pizza I had just ate. Zelle heard me throwing up and came into the bathroom.

"You aight?" he asked as my sickness came to a sudden stop.

"No," I gasped.

"Come on. It's aight." He embraced me.

"No, it's not I feel like a hoe."

"You ain't no hoe. Everybody make mistakes." He led me into his room. "Lay down. I'll call your mom and tell her you'll be home later."

I kicked off my shoes and climbed into his high, comfortable bed that was warm and soft. It seemed to welcome me. Within minutes I was asleep.

When I got home later that night, my mom was on the living room couch hugged up with some man. "Hi. Mom," I said as I walked passed them, headed to my room. I didn't feel like conversation. I collapsed on my bed, wanting only to lay there uninterrupted.

"Amina? Come meet Markus," she said excitedly peeking into my room. I didn't really feel like getting up, but I decided not to be rude. My mother seemed to be really interested in this man, which meant it was mandatory that I meet him. I followed her back into the living room.

"Markus baby, this is my daughter Amina."

"Hi." He gave a half-smile. He was dusty compared to my daddy. His complexion was dark chocolate. He wasn't a bad looking man, but he wasn't a good looking man either. My mom could have done a million times better as far as I was concerned. Her interest in him confused me.

"Hi," I replied not even giving one-third of a smile to his no-personality ass.

"How old are you?" he asked as if he actually cared, and as if I actually felt like answering the question.

"Seventeen," I replied.

"You look older. You're real pretty just like your mother." He gave me a whole smile this time. I still didn't like his vibe.

"Thank you," I said blankly.

"Markus is a lawyer at the office I work at." My mom informed me smiling proudly.

"Oh," was all I could say. Shit, he looked like a construction worker that had just came off his site to me. He wore a plain green T-shirt and a young fitting one at that. It was tucked into a pair off tight ass white wash jeans. On his feet were brown suede boots, and they certainly weren't fresh, nothing about him was fresh. He looked about 38 years old, and nothing about his appearance was lawyer-like. He was probably one of those shitty lawyers that couldn't win a case, even if their life depended on it.

I got sick of looking at him because he was so bummy. I

politely told them both good night, kissed my mom and went back to my room closing the door behind me. The only thing I could think of in the silence of my room was how I was going to break the news of my pregnancy to my mom, and most of all what Maurice would say. He didn't even know me, I didn't know him either. I turned on the TV and as soon as my mind was about set on having an abortion I saw a Pampers commercial. The innocent baby on the screen made me feel guilty for even having that thought. At this point I was more confused than I had ever been in my life. I had some real shit on my shoulders now and I knew it. I just didn't know what would result from it. I didn't want to see myself ten years down the road, following the same path as my mom trying to raise a child with no help. I wanted more.

Triple Crown Publications presents

Chapter 7

Sunday - August 3, 2003

My appetite was big enough for a whole army Sunday morning. Before I went to the kitchen to satisfy my craving of bacon, eggs, and hash browns, I knocked on my mom's bedroom door to ask her if she wanted some. She usually didn't sleep with her door closed, but I paid it no attention. I knocked softly two times, just loud enough for her to hear. There was no answer, so I slowly opened the door.

My stomach turned when I saw her lying in the bed with Markus. He was on his back with his big crusty feet sticking out of the covers. My mom was lying on his bare chest. The cover was low enough to see that she had no shirt on either. The room was sex-funky. I closed the door fast enough to keep my appetite.

I cooked enough for me and my mom. When I got done I placed her plate in the microwave, and carried my food into my room. I didn't bother to cook enough for Markus. I figured if she was so infatuated with that nigga, she would be willing to share her plate with him.

After I finished my food, I called Kelly. I wanted to get in touch with Maurice.

"You what?!" she yelled almost loud enough for my mom to hear from her room, when I told her I was pregnant. "By who?" she asked lowering her tone.

"I think its Maurice," I told her. Her whole attitude seemed to change.

"What make you think it's him?" she asked in a defensive tone.

"What the hell you mean? It gotta be him. I ain't fucked nobody else since early July. Plus, I missed my period this month. It was supposed to come on the tenth. You know that." It was true Kelly did know; we always came on at the same time. That's how it is when females are together a lot. It had been like that since we were about fifteen.

"You let him go raw?"

"I was drunk, Kelly."

"Well, Maurice the wrong nigga to get pregnant by. You see him one day but when he leaves he stay gone for about a year."

"What you mean? I thought he stayed in Mt. Auburn?"

"Girl, he left that next day. He told me he was gon' be gone for a while."

"You ain't got his number?" I asked desperately.

"Nope. I don't even know where in Mt. Auburn he stay at," she replied, "He make big money though, workin' for some big time nigga from Indiana, makin' lil runs and shit. That's what got him that Suburban he whippin' now," she continued. "I remember the days when Maurice wouldn't even think about sellin' no damn drugs," she laughed at the thought.

"Who is ole' dude he workin' for?"

"How would I know?"

I fell silent. Meanwhile, Kelly went into a dramatic story about some girl she wanted to fight. At first I was listening, but then my mind drowned out her voice. I was too busy trying to contemplate what in the hell I was going to do now.

"Huh?" I said when my mind finally came back to the conversation.

"Girl, was you even listening?"

"Yeah," I lied to stop her from taking me through the long drawn out story again.

"Anyways, Swag told me he seen you at the movies with yo brother?"

"Yeah."

"So, since when you have a brother?" She pushed trying to make something out of nothing.

"I just met him, and my Dad, two weeks ago."

"For real? How old is he and why ain't you tell me you met yo daddy? That's some deep shit."

"Twenty-two, and I don't know."

"Where they stay?"

"My brother stays in Mt. Auburn. My daddy lives in Indian Hill."

"Damn, Indian Hill?"

"Yup."

"You like them?"

"Yeah, it's kind of crazy all of a sudden havin' a brother and daddy around. But I like it, and they both got money. My dad owns that new Cadillac dealership in Tri-county. And Azelle whippin' dis fed ass Escalade."

"Bitch you lien! Every nigga I know go there to get shit put in their car so I know he paid."

"Hell yeah."

"Yo brother name Azelle?"

"Yeah."

"That's kind of cute. I'ma have to meet Azelle," she laughed.

"Aight. But I'ma lay back down so I'll call you later."

"Aight lil' momma," she giggled.

I didn't laugh. "Bye," I said hanging up. As soon as I drifted off to sleep, the phone rang.

"Hello." I answered half-sleep.

"Girl you pregnant!" The voice on the other end screamed in my ear like she had won a million dollars. Of course, it was Trina, she was the only person that would call me up yelling in my ear like she was half crazy.

"Yeah," I sighed, trying to give her the picture that I didn't feel like talking.

"By who?" she shouted.

Damn can this bitch talk any louder? I thought to myself. "His name is Maurice. You don't know him."

"Yeah, I heard he was Kelly's cousin."

"You heard right," I said honestly. There was no reason to lie.

"I know I'ma be the godmother!" she said excitedly like she honestly believed I would pick her for my child's Godmother.

"No. You know you bout to call me back, 'cause I'm trying to sleep," I said sounding annoyed.

"Aight." She hung up.

I couldn't understand why Kelly had to run her mouth about everything I told her. Ten minutes hadn't even passed before she went and told my business. I wasn't the slightest bit surprised when I got calls later on from Brell and Swag. Everybody seemed excited about the baby, but I was scared.

My mom finally came in my room to speak to me after Markus left. By then I was up and dressed. It was 3:30 p.m.

"Thanks for breakfast. It was good." She was late as hell, I had fixed her breakfast at 11 o'clock. But I wasn't pressing the issue. I had too many other things on my mind.

"You're welcome," I managed to spit out, even though I didn't mean it.

"You feeling better?" she asked concerned.

"I was sick yesterday not today, and you just now checking up on me? I don't need your concern now, so don't worry yourself about it."

She looked at me surprised at what I said. "Ok Mina. Your right, I'm sorry. I'll leave you alone," she replied softly as if I had hurt her feelings. She walked out leaving me feeling guilty.

Before I could run after her and apologize, the phone rang again for the thousandth time. "Hello." I answered irritably.

"Yeah, can I speak to Amina?"

"Who is this?"

"Kayne."

"Oh, what up?" My voice completely changed, it was like he melted me down.

"What's up ma, you aight?"

49

"Yeah. I'm cool, this damn phone been ringin' off the hook all day."

"Oh, you pimpin like that shorty?"

"Na. I ain't pimpin," I laughed. He had me in the palm of his hand from that point on. We talked about every little thing, including my pregnancy. He asked me if I was going to keep the baby. I told him I didn't know. He made it clear that my being pregnant didn't bother him, which was something that made him stand out.

Zelle called as soon as we hung up around eight o'clock at night. "I was just calling to check up on my lil' sister," he said after I asked him what was up.

"Thanks," I said.

"So, you told yo momma yet?"

"No."

"You gotta do it eventually. Might as well get it over with."

"Yeah, but I just don't know how."

"Want me to come over when you tell her?"

"Yeah."

"Aight. I'll be over tomorrow."

"Tomorrow?"

"Yeah, the sooner the better."

"What about Damen? Does He know?"

"Did you tell him?"

"No. I thought maybe you did."

"You ain't tell me to so I didn't."

Finally somebody I can trust, I thought to myself. "Well, I'll tell him eventually. But what time you coming?"

"Probably around four. You gon' be there?"

"Yeah. I'll be here, but she don't get off till five."

"I'll wait."

"Ok."

"Aight. So I'll see you then."

"Ok." I hung up hoping that would be the last conversation for the night, because I was exhausted and still hadn't gotten any sleep.

Triple Crown Publications presents

Chapter 8

Monday - August 4, 2003

When Zelle got to my apartment, we sat and watched videos until my mom got home. "Hi, Azelle. I didn't know you were coming over today," she said dropping her keys and purse on the kitchen table.

"Yeah. Just came through to chill with Mina for a while."

"That's cute," she laughed, stopping to look at us sitting on the couch together like she wanted to make it a Kodak moment.

"Yeah. I think Mina got some news for you." They both turned and looked at me. My whole body froze. I couldn't move. You could have waved a dick in my face and I still wouldn't have budged. My mom stared at me with an unsure look. Her good mood had quickly faded away.

"Um, I'm...um." I stared at my hands.

"You what?" she snapped.

"Pregnant," I mumbled, just waiting for her hand to come soaring across my face.

"What the fuck did I tell your ass?! Huh? I been tellin' you all these years to keep yo damn legs shut! And now look at you, 'bout to be stuck with a baby. How the hell you gone support a child? Tell me that."

"I'll get a job."

"Well good luck sweetie 'cause I ain't supportin' no baby."

I couldn't believe how she pretended like she didn't already see this coming. She let me do anything I wanted to so what did she expect? "You ain't got to. It ain't yours," I replied looking away.

"Damn right." She gave me a disgusting look, stormed off to her room and slammed the door behind her.

I tried not to cry, but I couldn't help it. I needed her support more than anything right now and she was completely through with me. Zelle hugged me as the tears trickled down my face. "If I would have just told him to put on a condom, I wouldn't be in this position."

"You fucked him raw?"

"Yeah."

"That's what liquor do to you."

"I know." I sat up to grab a tissue from the table next to the couch.

"And who the fuck is the boy that got you knocked up?" my mother asked startling me as she entered the room smoking a Newport. The only time she ever smoked was when she was really heated, and the smell really irritated me.

"His name is Maurice."

"So where you meet him, lil' hooker?"

I narrowed my eyes at her. "He's Kelly's cousin."

"Well, I pray to God she ain't pregnant too." She sat down at the kitchen table.

"You talked to Maurice?" Zelle asked.

"No, Kelly don't have his number and she don't even know where in Mt. Auburn he stay. She said he told her he would be gone a while, on runs and stuff. He supposedly work for some nigga in Indiana.

"Shit, I don't know where he live but I can find out. I'll probably run into him when I go down there, I always do."

"Mina." My mom looked at me with a sad expression. "I'm sorry for blowing up; I just didn't want you to end up like me but *I guess* it's already too late." She took another puff of her cigarette, and fell silent.

"Yeah," I sighed getting up to go into my room. I closed the door, and climbed into my bed, which had seemed to become my best friend for the last three weeks. Zelle came in behind me.

"You wanna go get some furniture for your room at my place? We can get a crib too, and whatever else you want." He asked trying to brighten my dull mood.

"I guess," I answered lying on my side, staring at the bare wall as he stood behind me.

"Is that a yes?"

"No, it's an I guess."

"Well, it's up to you," he said being patient with my attitude.

"Ok. Let's go." I got up, grabbed my purse and headed out the door without saying a word to my mom. Zelle stayed behind and explained where we were going.

Shopping was the perfect way for me to release my stress. I was surprised to find almost everything I needed in one spot, which was at Pier 1 at Rookwood Pavillion in Hide Park. I found the perfect canopy bed that had a gold tint, and a matching dresser. I bought a cute blue love seat to sit by the window, a silk royal blue and gold comforter, about ten sari print pillows, a white silk canopy, sheer blue curtains, a gold rimmed mirror and about twenty five candles of all different sizes. The total came to $4,267.80. Zelle planned to get a U-Haul and pick the furniture up that Thursday. He paid with a credit card and didn't seem at all phased by the price. We stopped at Home Depot for blue paint that I planned on sponging the walls with. Then it was to BW3's to eat. I stuffed myself with chicken wings, potato wedges and cheese sticks. Zelle laughed at how hungry I seemed to be. I thanked him for everything before he dropped me back off at the shit whole I called home.

When I got in, the first person I saw was Markus, sitting in front of the TV scarfing down a big bag of Doritos.

"Where's my momma?" I asked, rolling my eyes.

"She went to go pick up some Chinese food," he said, still stuffing his mouth with more chips.

"How long she been gone?" I asked looking at him in disgust.

"Why? You her keeper or something?" The question hit me hard.

"I can ask where my momma is! Who you think you are?" I snapped, sensing there would be drama ahead. But I didn't care, because obviously drama was what he wanted.

"I'm yo momma's man, that's who I am! I'm also her keeper, not you. So be a good little girl and keep yourself out of trouble, by keeping your mouth shut. And from what she's been telling me, you need to keep your legs shut too." His words shot at me like a nine mill. I couldn't believe my mom told this sick bastard that I was pregnant.

"I don't care what my momma told you. Seems to me like you need to get some fresh clothes, right along with some respect for your so-called *women's* daughter."

He shot me an evil-eyed glare. "Bitch you ain't shit. You ain't better than nobody 'cause yo daddy got money. I heard all about him. But look what you livin' in. You ain't shit but a stupid little hoe." My mom walked in as soon as he jumped up from the couch and raised his fist.

"Baby! What's going on?" She shouted dropping the food down on the table.

"Nothing baby, what took you so long?" He walked over to her and kissed her on the neck.

"You wouldn't believe how many people were in that place. You wanted shrimp fried rice right?" she asked looking worried that she might have gotten the wrong thing.

"Yeah," he answered glaring at me again, as my mom took the food out of the bag. I stood there speechless; she didn't even speak to me.

"What type of shit is this? This nigga just called me out my name and tried to hit me, which would have been the biggest mistake of his life, and you not gon' say shit about it?" I said approaching my mom.

"Amina. You better watch your damn mouth. Just 'cause you pregnant don't mean you gon' be talkin to me any kind of way. And Markus would never call you out of your name, or try to hit you. I'm sure he was probably just playing around with you. Lighten up," she looked at me and laughed.

"That's so fucked up," I said looking at the both of them shaking my head in disbelief.

"I said watch your damn mouth! And stop trying to mess up a good thing for me. I love him," she whispered.

"You don't love him. You don't even know him. You bein' dumb as hell!" I shouted as tears gathered up in my eyes. My own mother was choosing a man over me, and a crazy, abusive man at that.

"Shut Up! Don't say another fuckin' word to me. You're so selfish! That's what's so sad," she barked as Markus sat there with a satisfied grin on his face watching my mother in her own stupidity.

"You won't have to worry about me no more." My mother was going back to her old ways, taking sides with Markus the way she did with Tony. Instantly, I was taken back to the days in the Bronx where she would ignore me and make excuses for her good for nothing man.

"Good," my mom said returning to her food, and smiling in Markus's dirty face.

I went straight to my room to call Zelle's cell phone.

"Yeah?" he answered, lowering his music.

"You home yet?" I asked. Hoping he would pick me up.

"Na. I had to make a few stops. What's wrong?"

"I just got into it with my momma boyfriend. He started callin' me out my name, then call himself 'bout to hit me. That's when my momma came in and she act like ain't shit happen, talkin' 'bout she love him and don't mess up a good thing for her."

"Pack yo shit up. I'm on my way."

"Aight."

"And who is this bitch nigga she got?" Zelle's voice got louder.

"Some man named Markus, claim he a lawyer, but look like a damn bum."

"Look, just stay in your room and lock the door. I'll be down there in 'bout fifteen minutes."

"Ok."

"Just don't say nothing to either one of them, and don't tell 'em I'm coming."

"I won't." I did everything he told me starting with locking the door. Then I packed all my clothes. I threw all twenty-eight pairs of my shoes in a huge duffle bag and sat it against the wall with the rest of my bags. After packing my CD's, jewelry box and toiletries, everything was ready to go. My room didn't have much, and what it did have I didn't need. Like my TV and CD player, I figured Zelle would by me new ones. I didn't even have time to sit down before Zelle was at the front door. He knocked loud and hard.

"I know this girl ain't call no damn police." I heard my mom say on her way to open the door.

"Hi, Kayla." I heard Zelle say calmly.

"Hey. You back already?"

"Yeah. I stopped by to talk to ya boy right here." As soon as he said that I walked into the room. Markus got up from the table.

"What you want?" he said, standing up to Zelle as if he was supposed to be intimidating him.

My mom looked worried and confused. "What's going on? Yaw don't even know each other," she said stepping in between them.

"I don't mean no disrespect Kayla, but this nigga ain't 'bout to be callin my lil' sista out her name."

"What the hell you tell him Mina?" she turned to me.

"I told him what happened," I simply replied.

"Yeah. She told me exactly what happened so bring yo ass outside," Zelle said to Markus, walking out of the apartment to the front of the building.

Markus followed behind talking shit. "Little nigga, you don't want none. I'll squash yo young ass." Me and my mom stood on the sidewalk while Markus was shouting to Zelle from the door. He was drawing attention and everybody that was around stopped to look. Brell and Swag stood on the block watching with a few other niggas I knew and a dope fiend named Brenda who Swag always served. Zelle was in the middle of the street.

"Come here Mina." I walked over to Zelle. "Here, hold this for me." He took off his chain and watch, handing them to me. Markus walked into the street and I backed up. Zelle caught him to the jaw three times in a row, followed up by a hard punch in the nose that splattered blood. This caused my mom to start screaming, Markus came back with a sloppy uppercut that didn't phase Zelle at all. That was the only hit that Markus got in because before he could even swing again, Zelle had knocked him to the ground. He stomped him, and by this time my mom was on the sidewalk in tears. I had no sympathy for her or Markus.

"Get the fuck up nigga! Get up!" He shouted at Markus who was bleeding in the middle of the street.

"Aight, man," he moaned struggling to his feet. Zelle snatched him by the shirt and turned him towards me. "Apologize to her. Bitch ass nigga!" He shouted grabbing him harder after he tried to jerk away.

"I'm sorry!" He screamed looking into my eyes wishing for mercy from Zelle's tight grip. His nose was oozing blood along with his mouth. I said nothing. I felt no need.

"Don't let this shit happen again. Nigga, you respect my sister," Zelle continued.

"Ok, I'm sorry man," he cried desperate to be released. As soon as he thought he was free, Zelle slammed his head into the windshield of a broke down car that had been parked across the street for two months.

I handed Zelle his jewelry back and ran inside to get my

things before the police showed up. I knew it was already hot around my way. Swag came up to help me with my bags. I gave him the duffle bag, since it was the heaviest.

"So, you out of here, huh?" Swag asked, grabbing the bag.

"Yeah. My momma on that one way, choosin' that nigga over me."

"She townin' foreal."

"Hell yeah." We threw my bags in Zelle's back seat. I hugged Swag and Brell before they walked away trying to clear the scene. I looked over at Markus still trying to get his head out of the windshield, and my mom trying to help him. I walked across the street to say goodbye to my mom, I was hoping she would change her mind and beg me to stay. But before I could say anything, she turned away and hugged Markus.

"It's ok baby. It's just me and you now. Amina is gone for good," she said making sure she was loud enough for me to hear. I didn't say anything. I looked over to Zelle, who had heard her from across the street.

"Come on, you don't need her." He was right, I didn't need her. I was about to be a mother myself, and it would be cold and freezing in hell before I would choose any man over my child.

Chapter 9

Thursday - August 7, 2003

Kelly came over to help me paint. Zelle helped too. Kelly was crazy over Zelle. "He is so sexy," she told me when he walked out of the room to get the phone. I laughed. Kelly was always crushin' on somebody.

"Wait 'till you see Kayne," I told her, anticipating the moment when he would come over to help Zelle move my furniture in. The baby's crib was already there, I had bought it yesterday from a store that did same day delivery.

The whole time we were painting, Kelly was trying her hardest to catch Zelle's eye, while I was trying my hardest not to laugh. She bent over in her tiny white and blue RocaWear shorts that barely covered her ass. When that didn't work, she bumped her titties that were pushed up in her low cut tank top against him by "accident." But Zelle wasn't feelin' her. I tried to tell her to just chill out and let him approach her, but that wasn't Kelly at all. When she saw something she wanted, she went for it. We were definitely opposites in that department. I never was the type to approach a nigga; I always let them come to me. If they didn't I just figured they weren't for me.

When Kanye finally arrived he and Zelle helped me set the room up exactly how I wanted it. Kayne was looking so right in his fresh wife beater that revealed all six of his tattoos. As they carried my bed into the room, Kelly gave me a look of approval. Zelle didn't seem to notice Kayne's involvement with me until everything was complete and we all sat down in the living room. I sat next to Kayne, resting my head on his shoulder, of course Zelle quickly found a way to separate us.

"Come on, let's get this truck back. Then, I gotta go out to Circuit City to pick up this flat screen and CD player," Zelle said, tapping Kanye on the leg.

"Aight," Kayne agreed. He layed his hand on my thigh. "I'll be back aight?"

"Ok," I said leaning up from him. Kelly was indulged in some corny looking Lifetime movie that was in a climactic scene. Zelle grabbed his keys and left out before Kayne even got up. I knew he was mad, I just didn't really understand why.

By the time Zelle and Kayne got back, Kelly had left. I had just gotten out of the shower when they walked in my room carrying the flat screen TV. "Why ain't you close the door?" Zelle snapped when he noticed Kayne looking at me in my towel like he was wishing for me to just drop it.

"I wasn't expectin' yaw to get back that fast," I said innocently. They carried the TV back into the living room and waited for me to get dressed. After I oiled my whole body down, I put on a Baby Phat shirt and jean skirt that revealed my chest and legs perfectly. I left my feet bare to show off my pedicure I had gotten with Kelly two days ago. It was her treat, an attempt to release some of my stress. "I'm done," I said entering the living room, where Kayne and Zelle sat in silence. I sat down next to Kayne again.

"It took you that long to put that on?" Zelle commented looking at my outfit in disgust.

"You don't like it?" I smiled.

"Where the rest of it at?" Zelle screwed up his face.

"Zelle..." I laughed.

"I like it," Kayne chimed in.

"I bet. Just don't get too excited, ain't shit happenin," Zelle snapped

"Why not?" Kayne challenged him.

"Nigga, she seventeen," he said, as if I wasn't sitting right there.

"I know how old she is." I sat in silence as they went at it.

"So, like I said ain't shit goin' down."

"Aight. Chill out nigga. If you ain't tryna see me with yo sista it's cool she only got a few months anyway. Let's get this shit done. I gotta go." Kanye got up from the couch.

"What the fuck some months got to do with it?"

"She'll be eighteen." Zelle glared at him. Still heated, they both picked up the TV and carried it into my room. Next, they put the CD player in. After that, it was time to say goodbye to Kayne and for some reason it felt like it would be the last time I would see him, considering Zelle's disapproval of us being together. I thanked him for his help, we hugged, then I watched him walk out wishing I could go with him.

"Why you do that?" I asked as soon as the door shut.

"Do what?" Zelle asked casually as if nothing had happened.

"Try to tell him he couldn't talk to me."

"Look. I'ma just break it down for you right now, so we won't have no confusion later. Kayne is just like me. I known him since I was fifteen and he was thirteen. He ain't gon' fall in love with you and treat you like a queen and I know that's what you expectin'. I'm just tryna keep you from gettin' hurt. You my lil' sista and that's my job."

"Why can't you just let me find out for myself? I mean we ain't even together…yet."

"Ain't no *yet*. You won't be." The phone rang cutting off any further argument. "Hello," he answered sternly. "Yeah, we'll be there in a minute." He hung up. "Get yo shoes on, we goin over Damen's."

When we got to Damen's house, he greeted me with a hug. "I heard what happened with your mom and that fool. Don't worry, you'll be happy living with your brother."

Yeah, if he lighten up and let me live a little, I thought to myself.

"Come on let me give you a tour." He released me and led me to the left where there was an elegant sitting area. Zelle walked in the opposite direction. "This is my living room." I admired the cream colored couch that sat in the middle of the room with two matching chairs directly in front of it. In the middle was a glass table, and all of this sat on a white mink area rug laid perfectly on the cream marble floor. I loved the way the huge bay windows were everywhere. He led me further back, passing his dining room and chrome decorated kitchen. The next room we entered was the den.

"This is where me and my boys come and watch the game." There were two black leather couches. One on the left wall and one in front of the back wall's full-length bay windows. On the right wall was a bar. "I just bought this TV a few weeks ago," he said pointing to the huge flat screen that served as the room's focal point.

When we walked out of the den we met the steps. He showed me the other sitting room on the right side of the house before we went upstairs. It was exactly like the other one only it was decorated with a red couch and chairs and a red mink rug. "I call this the red room. People love this room, they always tell me they've never seen a room decorated in all red."

"Yeah, it's different, I like it," I confessed. Upstairs, the sides of the house were separated just like downstairs. First, we went left to Damen's room. It was huge with a lot of walking space. He had a king size bed and a big screen TV directly across from it. His bathroom had a hot tub and two sinks. "I love this," I said admiring the space he had. On the wall where his walk-in closet was, he had a brown leather couch that matched the room's color scheme perfectly.

"Thanks. I heard your room was being fixed up; I'll have to stop by and see it."

"Yeah, I love it. I can't wait to go to sleep in that bed tonight. It's so comfortable."

"Did you see the balcony?" He asked nodding towards the window. I walked over and opened the two window doors, stepping out onto the balcony. It offered a view of the pool in the back that had lounge chairs all around it. When I looked over to the left, I could see the back of the driveway where a black Mercedes G wagon was parked and next to it was an off-white Hummer.

"These your cars too? I thought you just had the BMW," I asked excitedly.

"The G wagon is mine and the Hummer is Zelle's, he keeps it parked over here." I couldn't believe how much money they had. I had never seen a G wagon up close before.

When we finished looking at the other three bedrooms, he showed me his movie theater in the basement that had a wide screen TV and ten big leather recliners lined up in two rows. Then, we were back upstairs in the kitchen. Zelle was sitting at the breakfast bar drinking a pop.

"Your house is so nice, who helped you decorate this? I know you didn't do it alone," I asked, pouring the Pepsi Damen had given me into a glass with ice.

"My girlfriend, Shayna, did all of this. She's on her way over now."

"Oh, ok."

"So when you gonna come work for me? I had to get rid of Camele. The front desk is yours, if you want it."

"Whenever you want me to." I didn't even ask why he fired Camele. It didn't matter, all that mattered was that I stole her job just like I said I would.

"Ok, why don't you start Tuesday. You can drive the G wagon."

"Foreal?!"

"Yes, under one condition. You'll have to stay over here for the week to drive it to work everyday. There's no room for it at Zelle's and I don't want it parked on the street."

"Alright," I agreed. Zelle still looked heated. I decided to test the waters. "Zelle, can you give me Kayne's cell phone number. I never got it; he always calls me from home."

"He must not want you to have it then." I was surprised he didn't completely go off on me. "I'm not gon' keep tellin' you the same thing. Here, do what you want." He slid his cell phone across the counter.

"Nevermind," I said sliding it back and rolling my eyes. "I wasn't that pressed anyway."

"What's going on with you and Kayne? Isn't he a little old for you," Damen joined in.

"You know him?" I asked surprised. If anything, I was expecting him to ask who Kayne was.

"Of course I know Keon. He's like my second son. He moved here with me and Zelle. He's from Chicago, too," he replied, revealing Kanye's real name.

Keon, that's kind of cute, I thought to myself. I wondered why he never said anything about being from Chicago. "Well, yeah we're talking. It's nothing serious yet. And *no* he is not too old for me. I'll be eighteen November seventh," I said sounding irritated instead of flattered by their over-protectiveness.

"Ok. Just be careful," Damen said backing down, sensing my attitude.

"Daddy, did I tell you I was pregnant?" I changed the subject to something else sense they wanted to be all in my business.

"No. By who? When did this happen?" he asked looking upset and confused.

"I found out a few days ago, and it's by this dude named Maurice. I don't know where he's at but he stay in Mt. Auburn somewhere."

"So you're sayin' he don't even know?" He was completely shocked.

"Nope." I took a sip of my soda. Anything negative he had to say I had already heard. I was getting used to all the questions.

"How's he gonna find out? Don't you have his number?"

"Nope." I didn't go into detail, it just wasn't necessary. But of course Zelle told it all, sharing his two cents.

"I know exactly who he is. Some lil' young nigga. He's one of her friend's cousins and she don't even know what street he stay on. I don't even know why yo momma let you hang with her. She too damn fast," he said referring to Kelly.

"Whatever," I snapped, and the room became quiet. Damen looked away, overwhelmed by all the info he just heard. Before any more verbal bashing could continue, I was saved by the bell.

"That's Shayna," Damen said, getting up to get the door. Shayna was a petite women, she looked about 32, at the most. She had a pretty smile. Her skin was flawless, just like mine, and she was light skinned, just like me. Our complexions were almost identical. She had a curvaceous shape like me also. "Amina, this is Shayna." Damen stood next to her with his arm around her shoulder.

"Hi," I greeted her.

"Hi, Amina. I've heard a lot about you," she sounded enthusiastic. "Damen has been talking about you since you all met. You're so pretty."

"Thank you." I had a big smile on my face. Her bright mood had a good effect on my shitty mood.

"Hi Zelle. How you doin'?" She started a conversation with him. While they talked, I scoped her outfit. She had on a white and black Bebe dress with wrap up sandals. She had a cute silver toe ring and a French pedicure just like me. On her left wrist was a diamond tennis bracelet, and on the other was a Guess watch. She had a huge diamond ring on her left middle finger. I was positive Damen was responsible for that weight, and also for the diamond heart necklace around her neck. Her hair was cut short, and it really complimented her face. I noticed her white Fendi handbag and keys to a Mercedes Benz she placed on the kitchen counter. It was obvious that she was high maintenance, just like me.

Chapter 10

Friday, August 15th 2003

I felt like a superstar driving the G wagon to work my first week. Sunday morning, Zelle dropped me off at Damen's. The best part about staying over there was being able to talked to Kayne whenever I felt like it. Later that morning, Shayna rode with me to go pick up Kelly and Trina, who were spending the night. We swam almost the whole day; the weather was perfect. That night, we watched gangster movies in the theater. Shayna was right along with us acting just like one of us. Trina and Kelly loved it. All three of us got to sleep in our own rooms. Monday was Labor Day so Damen grilled and some of his friends and employees came over. He wanted to show me off to everyone, and I can't lie, I loved every minute of it. Of course Zelle and Kayne were there. Zelle had his eye on me and Kayne the whole time; Kelly had her eye on Zelle and Trina was infatuated with him too.

Even though I hadn't worked for a whole two weeks, Damen paid me today. I counted the money he handed me; four fifties, two hundreds, two twenties, and a ten.

"Thanks." I grabbed my purse and headed for the door.

"Wait a minute!" He caught me right before I walked out.

"Huh?" I said turning around.

"I got something for you." He led me outside to the lot. "You're gonna love this."

When we got outside, Derrick, one of the workers I had been making eye contact with all week, pulled up in a royal blue Lexus coupe with 22-inch spinners right in front of me like he was picking me up. But instead, he got out and handed me the keys.

"Here. This you shorty," he said licking his lips before he walked away. Damen gave him a hard stare. I was speechless as I stared at the brand new Lexus parked in front of me.

"Daddy, is this really mine?" Jumping up and down, I hugged him.

"Yup, it's yours. You're about to be a mother. I think it's time you got your own car."

"Thank you. I really appreciate it." I rushed over to the beaming car in awe.

"You're welcome, get in." I thought I was dreaming when I opened the car door and I saw the lush black leather interior. The personalized headrest read *Mina*. The dashboard and steering wheel were maple wood. Installed was a MP3 player and above it a small TV just like Zelle's. "This plays DVD's. The DVD player is in the trunk, along with your speakers. They're fifteens, turn on the radio." I turned the radio all the way up. The base sounded good, it was like I had a club in my car.

"Yeah that's hot," I said getting out and hugged him again. "Thank you Daddy."

"Don't forget to thank your brother. He picked out everything."

"Ok," I said jumping back into the driver's seat.

"Wait 'till the kids at *school* see you in this," he grinned.

School, I thought to myself. I had forgotten all about school, and it was starting in three weeks. There was so much going on; my mind was on everything else. It dawned on me that I was going to be pregnant during my senior year. "Yeah," I said nervously. Giving him what I knew was a phony smile.

"And you know you can keep this as your after school job."

"Ok." Honestly, I wasn't really listening to what he was saying. All I know, I had a banging new car. Closing the door, I started the engine.

"Wherever you go, lock the doors and put the alarm on. Just push the buttons on your keys. And wear your seatbelt, or you'll get a ticket," he yelled through my rolled down window.

"I got it daddy," I waived and put it into drive.

"Ok, be safe." He backed away from the car and watched me drive off with a big Kool-Aid smile on my face.

My seat was low and comfortable. It felt more like a recliner than a driver's seat. I tested the speed not even realizing I was at a high risk of getting pulled over; especially being in Springfield Township. My first stop was to Tri-county mall for a new phone, then back to the hood. I had to show off my new car. After all, I was the hottest bitch in the 'Nati, hands down.

I traded my 3360 Nokia in for a new picture phone. I got eighty off the old Nokia, but I still had to put seventy on the picture phone, this covered my instillation fee too. I used the money I had saved up before leaving home. Zelle and Damen had been buying me everything, so I never had to spend one penny of my money. I had to admit I loved being spoiled, but it felt good making my money that I worked for. Even if it meant getting paid $450 every two weeks for doing basically nothing everyday from 10 to 5:30. Still, I worked for it. Shit, to me just getting up at 8:30 in the morning to be at work at ten was worth that $450.

After getting the hook up on the phone from one of Damen's friends (damn, I didn't realize how popular my father was) I was ready to leave the mall. I didn't stop in any stores because I was so anxious to go stuntin' in my new car. I didn't even get to my car before some nigga pulled up next to me in the parking lot trying to holla.

"Damn sexy. What up?" he asked leaning out the window of his black Suburban.

"What up?" I continued walking.

"My name Steelo. What's yo name, shorty?"

"Amina." I turned around to face him.

"Aight Amina, can I get yo number so we can hook up some-time, or you ain't feelin' me?" He gave me a sexy grin display-ing his six golds. He nearly melted me. I was already soaking wet just looking at his body in the fresh white wife beater he was wearing. His skin was a honey brown, which matched his eyes. His hair was perfectly tapered. Somehow I completely forgot about Kayne.

"I'm feelin' you." After we exchanged numbers, I told him "We can hook up right now if you want to." Since it was a nice day, and I was in a good mood, I decided to just give him what he wanted, pussy. *The hood can wait*, I thought. I leaned onto his window to give him a peak at my chest, and see if he was even worth my time. He seemed to be getting aroused by my actions. "You can follow me home," I continued.

"It's whatever ma. You got yo own place?"

"I stay with my brother in Corryville."

"Who is yo brother?"

"His name Azelle. You know him?"

"He drive a Hummer?"

"Yeah, and a Escalade."

"Yeah, that's my nigga."

"Oh foreal?"

"Yeah. So you gon' call home and make sure we gon' be alone?"

"I guess that would be a good idea." I laughed, now I was really flirting. I forgot all about the fact that it was Zelle's crib and how overprotective he was. When he didn't answer at home, I called his cell phone.

"Yeah?" he answered like he always did.

"Hey Zelle. I was just callin' to say thanks for picking out everything for my car." I was trying to make the conversation seem normal.

"You welcome. Where you at?"

"At Tri-county. I just came up here to buy a new phone. I'm 'bout to go home." I was hoping he would tell me where he was, and when he was coming home so I wouldn't have to ask.

"You need to start buyin' some school clothes. You start the first. You gotta go register Monday at eleven. Damen said he'll meet you down there."

"At eleven?" I dreaded having to go to registration.

"Yeah."

"Ok."

"I'll prolly be home about 8:30. I'm 'bout to hook up with this chick in Covington." I looked at my watch, it was 6:15. I noticed Steelo staring at me in my black Prada dress and matching handbag my grandma had gotten me during her recent trip to New York.

"Ok. I'll see you then." I quickly finished up my conversation with Zelle and closed my phone.

"So what's up?" Steelo smirked.

"He'll be home later on tonight, so come on."

"Where you parked?"

"Right here." I pointed to my coup, which was one car away.

"Damn shorty, that's you?"

That was just the response I was waiting for. "Hell yeah, that's me," I smiled.

"Aight."

Steelo followed me all the way back to my apartment. As soon as we got in, I took him straight to my room. Sitting on the bed, he began kissing on my neck, which was my spot. He came up to kiss my lips. After five minutes of non-stop kissing, we both came up for air. Needless to say, he was a good kisser. That was a big turn-on for me.

"Lay down." He pulled off my shoes and I laid across the bed; anxiously waiting for him to make his move and hoping it was the right one. Thank god, it was.

"I just wanna taste you," he said lifting up my dress, and pulling down my thong. By this time I was wet as hell, and hoping I wouldn't drown him to death. Slowly, he ran his tongue up and down the inside of both my thighs. Finally, after all the damn teasing, he reached my middle and licked my shit dry. He even blew on it right before I came. When he was done, I fell flat on the bed, catching my breath. I had been moaning for twenty straight minutes. Then, I got on my knees to return the favor. My jawbones felt like they were broken by the time he came, which was right after I pulled his dick out of my mouth. As bad as I wanted to fuck him, I knew it was best that I didn't. Besides, that wasn't my plan. It was only to give him pussy, and that's exactly what I gave him…to taste.

I looked at the clock on my phone. It was 7:35 p.m. "I'ma take a shower, you can chill in the living room for a while." I didn't want to make it seem like I was in a big hurry for him to leave. I got up to pick out some fresh clothes and underwear after he walked out. I made sure my shower was quick so that I would have Steelo gone before Zelle showed up. I also made sure I washed my mouth out thoroughly with Listerine. Within minutes, I was done and back in the bedroom.

"The shower feel good?" he asked as I sat down on his lap.

"Yeah. You should have got in with me." I wanted to kiss him so bad.

"You can kiss me; I went in Zelle's bathroom and washed my mouth out." He kissed me before I could kiss him. "It's yo pussy anyway," he laughed.

"I know."

"I betta roll out before he get home though. I'll call you."

"Ok." I got up from his lap.

"Good shot on the dome ma." He gave me one last sexy grin.

"Oh, you know. A favor for a favor," I said standing in the doorway and watching him walk to his car. Since I was alone with nothing to do, I called Kayne to tell him I was home. Then I called Kelly to tell her about my car.

"Girl, why yo brother be on that?" she asked after she had gotten overly excited about the news of my car.

"What you talkin' 'bout?" I asked confused.

"He can't talk to me, but he all in Amber shit."

"Amber who?"

"You know who I'm talkin' 'bout, Amber from Covington. They rode through the strip yesterday; he had her in the car and that otha bitch she always be with. I think her name Neesha."

"What?" I was still confused.

"Girl that's what I said. Why her gutty ass?"

"I'ma have to talk to him about that. How old is she anyway?"

"Like 19 or 20."

"Oh, what about Neesha?"

"I don't know about her."

"Who was you on the strip with?"

"Trina, we went over there after registration."

"Yaw registered already?" My mouth dropped. *Damn, where was my head?*

"Yeah when you goin'?"

"Monday."

"You can go tomorrow. Saturdays its open from nine to 11."

"Ok."

"I'll call you back. This Shawn beepin' in." Kelly said goodbye.

"Ok."

Saturday – August 16, 2003

I woke up at seven in the morning to Zelle yelling at somebody on the phone.

"Man, I don't know what the fuck happened. But I'ma find out. I'll get back at you in a minute." I got up and went into the living room to see what was going on.

"What's wrong?" I asked half asleep.

"I had ten stacks in a Jordan shoe box on the second shelf in my closet. It was covered up with sweaters and hoodies, so how it's missing, I don't know." I knew Steelo had to be the one who did it, but I wasn't sure because he told me they were cool.

"Damn," I said not knowing what else to say. I wanted to change the subject and ask about Amber but I knew it wasn't the right time.

"Amina, I don't mean to be accusing you of shit, but did you have anybody in my house yesterday?"

Damn, this nigga always seems to know what to ask, I thought, dreading having to answer. "Well…yeah I did, but you know him. He said he was cool with you."

"Who?"

"His name is Steelo."

"What the fuck?! You had that bitch ass nigga in my house? What the hell wrong with you?" He was so loud the people on the first floor could probably hear him.

"He said you was his nigga?" I said helplessly.

"I can't believe you so naive! You don't believe everything people tell you, especially no nigga."

"I'm sorry Zelle." I felt so bad.

"Yeah, you real sorry. You want me to treat you like you grown but you act like a lil' ass girl!" His harsh words made me feel about small as an ant in the middle of New York, New York. I couldn't say anything at all. I just stood there listening as he went on and on.

"I needed that money. It wasn't even mine, it was a loan from one of my niggas until I got my shit in. And I ain't the type of nigga to fuck up and not pay niggas back."

"I said I'm sorry Zelle."

"Don't have no more niggas in my house, and I mean that shit!" he yelled. I walked back into my room, closing the door behind me to drown out his voice. A few minutes later he left out, slamming the door behind him.

I laid in my bed feeling remorse for my stupidity. When the house phone rang, it took me a long time to decide whether I wanted to answer it or not. But I eventually did.

"Hello?"

"Is Zelle there?" A female voice asked.

"He ain't here. Who is this?"

"Amber. Who is this?"

"His sister. What you fuckin' with my brother for?"

"What you mean, what for?"

"Exactly what I said bitch, what for?"

"For the same reason you fuckin' with his enemies. Suckin' they dicks and shit."

Her words shocked the hell out of me. "What the fuck you talkin' bout?" I asked, even though I knew there was no point in denying it.

"You know what I'm talkin' about. It's all over. Steelo came back over here telling all his niggas he got Zelle's lil' sister to suck his dick."

"Came back over where?"

"Covington, bitch. He live right over here by me."

I wanted to go through the phone and kill her. But I stayed calm. "Did he tell you he ate my pussy?" I asked in a taunting tone.

"Yeah, and he said it tasted dirty," she said coldly before hanging up.

I couldn't believe what I had just heard. Even though I didn't know anyone in Covington, I knew that I had tainted Zelle's name by fucking around with his enemies. I felt like a nasty hoe, which was exactly what I had become.

After lying in the bed a while longer, I decided to get up, get dressed and go to registration. It was already 9:30 a.m.

In the shower I stood directly under the steaming hot water, trying to release my stress. I was drying off in the bathroom, when I heard my cell phone ring. I rushed into my room to answer it.

"Hello?" I answered.

"What up baby?" Kayne's voice said. I didn't know how I could ever face him again after what happened. As close as he and Zelle were, I was sure he had heard.

"Nothing. Just got out the shower."

"You sound like you been cryin." He sounded concerned.

"Oh."

"You ain't gon' tell me what's wrong?"

"I'm fine," I insisted, refusing to tell him that I was crying over what had happened with another nigga.

"It's cool. I already know what's wrong. Don't worry 'bout it. I got that nigga and Zelle will get his money back."

"Kayne. I'm sorry," I pleaded.

"Don't be sorry. I ain't mad, everybody fucks up. I just wanna know when you gon' stop fuckin' with these lames and get with me?"

"I don't know. You know Zelle trippin'. Plus, I'm pregnant and shit."

"I talked to Zelle he said he was gon' chill out, and I thought we talked about the whole thing with you bein' pregnant. Didn't I tell you that didn't matter to me?"

"Yeah, but-"

"But what? You ain't tryna fuck with a nigga for real?"

"What? No, it ain't that…"

"Then you my girl now. You belong to me now. Right?"

"Yeah," I answered. I couldn't argue anymore. Fuck all those other niggas. Kayne was it.

"Good. So, what you into today?"

"I gotta go register for school, they close at eleven o'clock."

"You ain't gotta have a parent?"

"Yeah, Damen is supposed to meet me down there."

"You went shopping yet?"

"No, not yet."

"Why don't you let me take you to registration. Then I'll take you shoppin' afterwards."

"You ain't gotta do that. I got enough clothes to last me for a while."

"Well, you 'bout to have more. Get dressed. I'll be there in twenty minutes."

"Ok."

At Kenwood Mall I shopped at BeBe, Express, Guess, Wet Seal, Gap, Dillard's, Coach, Steve Madden, Journey's, Victoria's

Secret, and MAC. We had to make two trips to the car, there were thirty bags total.

After the shopping spree, we ate at Outback. I almost fell asleep on the way back home. It was a quiet ride, except for the front TV that was tuned to BET. I guess Kayne sensed that I was tired, so he spared me any conversation or loud music.

"I see you been shopping," Zelle said, as me and Kayne hauled all of my bags into the house. He seemed to be in a good mood, and he didn't seem mad at me anymore.

"Yup," I smiled.

"You bought the whole mall," he laughed.

"Almost." I walked over to kiss Kayne. "Thank you boo."

"It's nothin' baby."

"I'm gonna lay down." I walked towards my room.

"Hey, Mina." Zelle walked over to where I was standing in my bedroom doorway.

"What's up?"

"Look, I'm sorry for going off on you like I did earlier. I know you didn't know he was gon' get me for my money. I can't blame you."

"It's ok." I was relieved that I could put the whole situation behind me.

I didn't even take my things into my room before I collapsed on my bed. I turned on the TV; some corny detective show was on. The detectives looked like a cross between Inspector Gadget and Batman. When I finally got tired of looking at it, I turned it off without even bothering to search for something decent to watch. My room was finally nice and quiet. So quiet, I was able to overhear Kayne and Zelle's conversation.

"You takin' care of my lil' sister?" Zelle asked like he would have shot him right on the spot if he was mistreating me.

"Yeah. Nigga what you so noided about?"

"It's just that she's young. I don't want her doin' no shit she don't need to be doin.' It's bad enough she pregnant."

"Don't worry 'bout it. I ain't gon' fuck up."

"That's all I wanted to know."

"Shit, you worried 'bout me and shit. Who you fuckin' with?"

"Nobody foreal, some bitch name Amber. Stay over there in Covington."

"Where you meet her at?"

"Over there. Last week and shit."

"So, what up? You hit?"

"Nigga, she a gutty. Fuck the same day, I hit the same hour I met her."

"Damn."

"Man, fuck this. I can't talk to yo ass 'bout no hoes no more'. You wit my sister now."

"What that gotta do with shit?"

"I can't ask you the same things."

"Why not," Kayne laughed. "I'm still yo boy."

"Man, shut the fuck up," Zelle said, shaking the thought of Kayne and I fucking.

"Damn, chill out nigga." Kayne went to the kitchen to get something to drink.

"You talked to Tah?" Zelle yelled.

"He ain't got back from Louisville yet, but when he do I got you."

"Cool. I'm gon' get that nigga Steelo tonight. You with me?"

"Hell yeah? Where at?" Kayne walked back into the living room where Zelle was turning on the Playstation.

"Covington, where else. I got a drop to make. Dude gon' have him where I'm makin' my drop at."

"What you payin' dis cat?"

"Nothin' for real. A stack. He a bitch. I milked his ass."

"He from over there?"

"Yeah."

"What time we leavin'?"

"I told him to meet me at 10:30?"

"Where at?"

"Same place I always make my drops at over there."

"Over on East 13th?"

"Yeah."

"Aight." The conversation ceased and Kayne opened the door to my room. "A, you sleep?" He walked over to my bed.

"I was," I lied.

"Oh, my bad." He started kissing me on my neck, but I pushed him away.

"Stop, let me go back to sleep," I said sounding frustrated. Of course it wasn't real frustration, just an act to keep him from thinking I was awake and heard him and Zelle talking. "I'll call you later." I rolled over, turning my back to him.

"Aight. I'ma leave you alone."

"Shut up. You shouldn't have woke me up," I chuckled.

"Me and Zelle gotta go make a drop over in KY, around ten. It's 8:40 now; if you wake up and we gone, you know where we at. So, don't cry," he said sarcastically, rubbing my back like I was a baby.

"Ok." I giggled.

Even though Steelo deserved to be shot, I wanted to stop Kayne and Zelle from doing it because I was worried something would go wrong. If Zelle went to jail, I would be heartbroken. And even if Kayne got locked up I would have been sick, because even though we weren't in love or anything yet, he supported me and respected me like no nigga, besides my brother, had done before.

Chapter 11

Sunday - August 17, 2003

It was three a.m. and Zelle and Kayne hadn't even called. I had been sitting up waiting for them to come back since the minute they left, and I was starting to panic. I had called Zelle's phone twice and Kayne's three times. Neither one answered. All kinds of things were running through my head, from them being arrested, to getting shot by Steelo and his niggas. I even thought about driving over to Covington to look for them, but I was sure they weren't still on East 13th. After waiting for another ten minutes the phone rang. I answered on the very first ring.

"Hello?" I said anxious to hear one of their voices on the other end.

"Mina, Guess what?" It was Kelly. I immediately became agitated.

"I'll call you back later." I was about to hang up.

"Wait!" She yelled before I hit the end button.

"What?" I asked hoping she wouldn't go into one of her dramatic stories that had become her trademark throughout the past seven years.

"I talked to Maurice."

"So, did you tell him?"

"Yeah."

"What did he say?"

"He said ok."

"Ok what?" I was really aggravated now.

"Just ok. He ain't say shit else."

"What the fuck is 'ok' supposed to mean? You ain't told me shit." I heard someone click in on the other end.

"I don't know Mina. You gon' have to talk to him. I gave him both your numbers," She replied calmly.

"Whatever. Just fuck it." I hung up before she could respond and clicked over to the other end.

"Hello?"

"Mina, this Zelle-"

"Where the hell yaw been?" I snapped cutting him off.

"My bad. My phone went dead."

"What about Kayne? I called his three times."

"His did too. We had a couple drops to make, but I saw ya boy Maurice."

"I just talked to Kelly. She said she told him and he said ok. 'Ok,' that's all he said Zelle was ok. What's that supposed to mean?"

"Don't worry 'bout it. I beat his ass. I told him you was pregnant too and he came at me all wrong so I took care of him, and you know Kayne jumped in. We threw his body in the dumpster."

"Damn did you kill him?"

"I ain't discussing that shit right now."

"Why you just now callin'?"

"I went ova this broad house."

"Who Amber?"

"Na, not her. How you know 'bout her anyway?"

"She used to always be down the way, and she was the one who called and told me about Steelo. I can't stand her. Why you mess with her?"

"I don't mess with her she just a good piece of ass."

"Whatever. Was Kayne with you over this *broad's* house?"

"Yeah. He was sittin in the livin' room."

"With who?" I started to get jealous.

"By himself. What, you think I would let him fuck with someone else? Don't act dumb."

"Well, was this female more important than me? Why couldn't you call?"

"There you go actin' like a lil' girl again. You'll be eighteen soon. You don't need me to call and check on you. I figured you was sleep anyway. I'll be home in a lil' while." He hung up without giving me a chance to respond. But I was relieved to know that he and Kayne were on their way home.

While I was lying on the couch, the phone rang again.

"Hello?" I answered in a more calm tone than I would have ten minutes before.

"Mina?" It was Zelle again.

"What?"

"If some nigga named Tino come over there, give him that Timberland bookbag hanging on the back of my closet. That's the nigga I owe money to."

"Ok."

"But don't let him in. I don't want him in there with you."

"Aight Zelle. Damn!" I was getting tired of his over-protectiveness. Just two minutes ago he was reminding me that I would be officially grown in a couple months.

"You betta chill out." He scolded me like he was father rather than my brother.

"Whatever." I rolled my eyes.

"If he ain't got a python tatted on his right arm, it ain't him. Check, cause niggas sneaky. You see what Steelo did.

"I got it."

"We'll be there in about twenty minutes."

"Bye." I hung up the phone. I was a little nervous about Tino coming over. I didn't want to disappoint Zelle again by trusting someone I shouldn't. This time I was going to try to keep things under control, and I figured Zelle would get home before Tino showed up anyway. But as soon as that thought crossed my mind, there was a knock at the door. I ran in Zelle's room to get the bookbag. Whatever was in the bag had to be a big deal because of the warning Zelle just gave me. Nosey, I peaked inside and saw stacks of hundreds. I definitely had to make sure it was Tino before I handed it over. Tino was tall and dressed in all black—black Sean John T, shorts and black Air Force Ones. I could tell he was big time because he was fresh. He was serious looking, but in a sexy way. His hair was tapered with waves like Zelle's and he wore a phat ass diamond earring in his ear like Kayne. His complexion was the same as mine. When I opened the door after looking through the peephole, he looked me up and down like a piece of meat. His eyes were immediately drawn to my thick thighs that were exposed in my light blue terry cloth Bebe shorts that I wore with a matching logo back out.

"You Tino?" I asked drawing his attention away from my body.

"Yeah."

"Let me see your right arm." He lifted up his right sleeve revealing the python that was tattooed on his arm. He definitely had a body, but I told myself I wouldn't get caught up with him. He was here for business, so I would keep it that way. Plus, I was officially with Kayne now.

"You a smart one," he commented, after he made sure that I had seen his trademark tattoo.

"I know." I said picking the bag up from behind the door. I tried my hardest not to be seductive as I bent over, but his eyes were planted on my ass. *Damn, why did I do that?* I thought to myself wishing I had just made him wait while I ran to get the money.

"Aight sexy." He placed the bag over his shoulder.

"So, you Zelle's girl?"

"His sister." I stood halfway behind the front door, ready to close it and go back to my business.

"Where he at?"

"On his way home."

"Can I come in and chill with you? I need to talk to him anyway. I was just gon' wait for him to get here."

I didn't know what to say. I didn't want to sound childish by telling him Zelle told me not to. "Yeah. You can chill, but that's all. I got a nigga." As those words came out of my mouth, I knew I was dead wrong. I started to change my mind, but before I could open my mouth and tell him to go wait in his car, he had brushed past me and took a seat on the couch.

Not knowing what to do, I sat down next to him and he moved in closer to me. I was starting to feel uncomfortable, but I just tried to ignore him by gluing my eyes to the TV.

"Why don't you take off that shirt, and let me see them big ass titties," he said, reaching for the tie to my halter-top.

"Hell na!" I pulled his hands off of me.

"What you mean hell na, why not?"

"Cause I just told you I gotta nigga. You need to leave." I got up off the couch and looked at the door, to give him a hint. He got up, but he didn't leave. Instead he tackled me onto the couch.

"Stop!" I screamed, trying to push him off of me. He was so heavy, there was no use. He covered my mouth with his left hand, and pulled down my shorts with his right. I kept screaming even though I knew no one was around. The people downstairs were out of town. I don't think anyone would have heard me anyway.

"Bitch, shut the fuck up." He smacked me so hard, I was sure his handprint was visible on the left side of my face. I kicked him in the balls. He removed his hand from my mouth and punched me. Blood splattered from my nose and mouth at the same time. After that, I felt no need to scream anymore. He was already inside of me. I laid there helpless as he fucked me. I stared at the clock above the TV while he forcefully pushed in and out of me. Ten minutes passed and he was so into his orgasm that he didn't hear Zelle opening the door, but I did.

Before he realized they were there, Zelle and Kayne had grabbed him off of me, and started catching him with body shots one after another. When he fell to the floor, they stomped him until he was unconscious.

As I watched them jump him, I felt like beating my own ass for not listening to Zelle. They picked him up and carried him outside. I don't know what they did with him because I was in so much pain, I couldn't even get up to look out the window.

"Why the hell did you let him in here; do you ever listen?!" Zelle yelled as soon as they came back in.

"Don't yell at her," Kayne said pulling up my shorts, picking me up, and carrying me to my bed. "It's gon' be aight baby. I got you."

I wanted to say something but I couldn't. My mouth hurt too much to speak. Zelle came in with a warm rag to clean the blood off of my face. "We gon' get you to the hospital, just hold on aight?" I nodded in substitution of words. Zelle helped Kayne pick me back up. When he was sure that Kayne had me secure in his arms, Zelle let go, allowing Kayne to carry me alone. I couldn't believe how calm Kayne was after I had just had a nigga in the house. He even calmed Zelle down for me. Maybe he thought Tino forced his way in. I don't know, all I know is that I was lucky. I knew I didn't deserve a nigga like him, or a brother like Zelle. I was just plain stupid.

I had learned my lesson. I would never go against what Zelle told me again. Kayne sat in the back seat with me. My head was in his lap. The whole ride he was telling me to hold on and that we were almost there. I felt dizzy, and my body was weak. I knew Tino had fucked my insides up, but if he had killed my baby, I was going to kill him.

Once inside the emergency room at Christ Hospital in Mt. Auburn, they ran two tests on me. After that, they transferred me to another room. Zelle, Kayne, and I sat and watched TV awaiting the results. Zelle sat on one side and Kayne on the other. Damen rushed in ten minutes later with a bouquet of roses. I guess Zelle had called him while I was being tested.

"Hey baby. How you doin?" He kissed me on the cheek, laying the roses in my lap. I didn't respond. Instead, I looked him in the eye and tears fell one by one. "Don't cry, everything is gonna be all right. You gonna be out of here soon," he said leaning over to hug me.

The doctor came in holding some papers with a sincere smile on her face. "Amina, we have good news and bad news," she announced, catching everyone's full attention.

"What?" Kayne asked anxiously.

"There was damage done, but you didn't lose the baby."

"How didn't I lose the baby, if there was damage done?" I asked. I felt like someone had shoved a pole inside of me, and that alone had to kill the baby. Of course I was happy to hear it didn't.

"You hear that? I told you you was gon' be ok. You pulled through," Kayne said kissing me.

I only smiled.

"The bad news is that your back wall was broken and it will take some time to heal. You will have bleeding for the next week."

"So can we take her home? Or does she need to stay here?" Zelle asked.

"We recommend that she remain in the hospital for at least two more days."

"Ok," Zelle replied. He finally looked relieved. I could tell he had really been worried by the look on his face while we were waiting on the test results.

"And for the sake of her fractured jaw, she doesn't need to eat any solids for a week. Only soups, no sodas just water and cranberry juice. It will help clean out your system."

"I didn't catch any kind of disease did I?" I asked nervously.

"As of right now all of your STD and HIV tests came back negative. But it's always good to drink cranberry juice. You should make it a regular thing."

"Alright," I said relieved.

"Thank you," my father said, shaking the doctor's hand.

Zelle sat back down next to me. "I was worried 'bout you kid," he said, looking me in the eyes. "You gotta start listenin' to me."

"I will; I'm sorry. He told me he needed to talk to you, and just wanted to wait for you to get home," I confessed crying.

"It's aight. Just go to sleep," he said taking my hand. Kayne and Damen were looking at me, their eyes full of worry. I closed my eyes, to go to sleep. It was 6:30 in the morning. I had been up for hours, and after experiencing a crazy night, sleep sounded good.

Triple Crown Publications presents

Chapter 12

Tuesday - August 19, 2003

I was tired of all the doctors and nosey nurses, I was ready to go home. The swelling in my fractured jaw was down and I was able to walk around without any help. Kayne and Zelle were with me around the clock. Kayne stayed with me both nights, while Zelle came by every morning and stayed until about midnight each night.

Trina and Kelly came to visit my first day here; they were upset that I wasn't going to be with them on the first day of our senior year. Brell and Swag came by on Monday. They swore up and down they would kill Tino, but I just told them that it was already taken care of. They made me promise that I would come and smoke with them as soon as I got out, just like I used to. Of course I agreed. I figured one joint wouldn't hurt my baby.

As I was getting dressed to go home, I glanced in the mirror and was horrified by my own face. My bottom lip was swollen, and my right eye had a maroon ring-shaped bruise around it. After one look at myself, I tried not to look again.

Kayne knocked on the door. "You ready baby?" He peaked his head inside.

"Almost." I was so embarrassed that everyone had seen me

so fucked up, especially Kayne. I knew all the makeup in the world wouldn't help. I would just have to let it heal.

"Ok." Kayne went back into the hallway.

As I was turning to leave the bathroom, I caught another glimpse of myself. I broke down in tears. I couldn't believe my life had gotten so out of order. It seemed like ever since the night I got into it with my mom and Markus, everything was going downhill. I was starting to really miss her. I thought about calling her but my pride wouldn't let me. I knew she didn't have Damen's number but I wondered if she even wanted to get in touch with me. *If she wants to talk, she'll call. Damen's listed in the phonebook,* I told myself.

When Kayne heard me crying, he came in and took me in his arms. I cried for a while. He didn't say anything at all. But I didn't even care, because I didn't need him to say anything. His holding me was enough.

After I dried my eyes, and pulled myself together, I was ready to go. On our way out of the hospital to the car, I walked with my head down toward the floor.

"Keep your head up. You ain't gotta try to hide your face, you still the best lookin' female in the world," he said, trying to build my confidence. But in my opinion, I was ugly and couldn't stand to be looked at.

"You just sayin' that 'cause your my boyfriend."

"No, I'm not saying it because I'm your boyfriend. I'm saying because it's the truth. I would never lie to you. Didn't I tell you that you could trust me?"

"Yeah," I mumbled. As I slowly climbed into the car, I remembered what my mother had once told me, *"Trust is the best thing you can have in any type of relationship."* I knew she was right, but I wasn't sure if I trusted Kayne yet.

As soon as Kayne drove off, his cell phone rang.

"Yeah," he answered, just like Zelle always did. "What?" His voice sounded upset and surprised. "What time?…From the crib?…Damn." At this point, I had a pretty good idea of what was going on. There was a long pause. "Aight." He hung up the phone.

"What's wrong?" I asked.

"Zelle got knocked. They raided the apartment."

"For what? Killing Steelo?"

"Na. Drug trafficking, and drug possession."

"How much?"

"He said he got caught with seven O's."

"So, he got away with the shooting?"

"Shit, hopefully."

"They talking ten years? Ain't no bail?"

"I don't know I gotta see what's up."

Before I could respond, my cell phone rang. "Hello?" I answered pissed off.

"Damn. What's wrong?" It was Kelly, the last person I wanted to hear from.

"Ain't you supposed to be at school?" I yelled.

"I am. I'm on my cell phone. Girl, remember how you told me about that nigga Steelo?"

"Yeah." I wished she would just get to the point.

"Well, I heard on the news last night that he got shot six times. That was Amber's cousin. She was down on Vine last night with Freddy ugly ass, cryin' all over him and shit."

"Oh well, he deserved it." I said acting like I knew nothing about Steelo's death.

"Yeah, he did you so wrong, and my baby Zelle," she laughed.

"Come on tell me the truth. Did Zelle do it?"

"Hell na, I ain't even know he was dead," I lied. I knew telling Kelly would turn Zelle's sentence from ten years to life. "But he beat Maurice ass I know that."

"I heard. Why you gotta attitude?"

"Cause I'm sick of yo big ass mouth. You don't know how to shut the fuck up! As soon as I told you I was pregnant, my phone was ringin' off the hook with ma'fuckas callin' me askin' if it was true. Now you calling me from school asking if my brother killed ol' boy. So since you can't ever keep yo damn mouth shut, just do me a favor and don't call me no mo'."

"What the fuck?! That shit is so old. If you gon' try to go off on somebody you need to come better than that." Heated, I hung up on her and threw my phone inside my purse.

"I'm guessin' that was Kelly," Kayne said calmly.

"Yeah. That was her big mouth ass."

"That's how most females are. You should know that."

"I do."

"I meant to tell you, Zelle said he loves you. He wants you to visit when he's allowed visitation."

"That was him that called?"

"Yeah."

"Why ain't he call me."

"He only got one phone call. He said he didn't know if you was checked out of the hospital already."

"So Damen don't know either?"

"No. We're headed to the dealership now."

"Kelly just told me that Steelo and Amber was cousins."

"Damn. If she find out 'bout Zelle she gon' snitch. I know it."

"I'll kill that bitch. I swear at God."

"Baby, just chill out we gon' get him out. I don't know how, but we will."

"Ok," I said taking a deep breath and trusting his words.

"Come on let's go tell pops what's up," he said, pulling into the parking lot of the dealership.

"Yeah, ok." I got out of the car, wishing this was all an nightmare that I would wake up from.

In the one month that I knew Damen, I had never seen him panic like he did when Kayne told him about Zelle. "I gotta go. I gotta get the hell out of here," he said, pacing back and forth in his office.

"What you mean?" Kayne asked with a puzzled look on his face.

"I gotta leave. I know if they got Zelle, I'm next. How you think I started this business? Not all of the money came from the old dealership. I bought the house and cars with that money, you know that," he said looking at Kayne.

I didn't say anything. I just sat down and put my face in my hands. I didn't know if things could get any worse. I didn't speak to my mom anymore, I had just cut off my best friend and my brother was facing ten years in jail. Now it looked like my father, who had just walked back into my life, was leaving again.

"Damen, you ain't gon' get caught. The Feds ain't onto you. You got visible means of income," Kayne said reassuringly.

"I ain't takin' no chances. I'm leaving. I don't feel comfortable here anymore." Damen started gathering papers.

"Do what you feel you need to do." Kayne shrugged his shoulders and looked over at me.

"Amina?" Damen knelt down next to me, pulling my hands away from my face. When I looked him in the eye, he seemed about ready to cry.

"What?"

"I'm so sorry, but I have to go back to Chicago. It's what's best for me. You can stay here, I'll get you an apartment, or you could go with me. But you can always call your mother or your grandma."

"I wanna stay," I told him. I didn't feel like trying to persuade him to stay, and I definitely wasn't up to leaving Kayne.

"You goin' back home?" Damen asked me.

"I don't know what I'm gonna do."

"She can stay with me," Kayne said.

"Wait, what about all my stuff at Zelle's?" I was desperate to have all my fits back.

"I'll take you shopping again," Kayne assured me. "We can't get it back now." He hugged me.

"Alright. She can stay with you but I want you to start school when your face heals." Damen kissed me on the forehead.

"Yeah," I answered blankly.

"I'll need you to come in to work this week, to help me get everything together," he added. I just looked at him with no expression.

"We'll be here tomorrow at ten," Kayne told him, answering for both of us.

"I want both of you to pick out an extra car free of charge."

"How generous," I said sarcastically.

"You always need a get away car the police don't know about," he continued. I didn't say anything, but I knew he was right. I just hoped no more shit would go down.

Triple Crown Publications presents

Chapter 13

Wednesday - August 20, 2003

First thing I did when I got to the dealership was pack all the files from my desk and Damen's office into boxes. Damen made calls arranging for all of the cars to be picked up Friday morning. He said he didn't feel like having a going out of business sale. It would take too long to get rid of everything; he even sold his G wagon and Zelle's Hummer. That's how he made up for the money he lost by giving me and Kayne free cars. Some rich kid, who lived out in Indian Hills, not too far from Damen, talked his parents into buying the Hummer for $48,000. As for the G wagon, another neighbor bought it for his wife for the same price.

When it was time for me and Kayne to choose cars, I chose the blue Escalade EXT that I'd been eyeing since day one. Kayne picked a black Cadillac CTS. I liked it because it was classy. After the windows of both of our cars were tinted, and the 22's were added to my car, all of the workers loaded up everything in the garage until it was completely empty. Damen would give all of the workers their checks that Friday, including me.

We rode to a storage garage near the dealership to put our extra cars away. Damen drove his Benz; I drove Kayne's Yukon. Kayne drove his new Cadillac, and Derrick helped by driving my truck. There was enough room for three cars in the garage. It was a good spot, because it was isolated. Damen handed Kayne a key.

"You can make Mina a copy, I only have one. Don't store any drugs in here unless you really need to."

"I got you." Kayne slipped the key in his pocket.

"Nobody will mess with them out here. Still, check on them at least twice a month." While Damen was going over all the rules with Kayne, I stood next to my truck with Derrick.

"It's fucked up that Damen's leaving. I won't get to see you no more." He moved in closer to me.

"Yeah." I agreed nervously as I glanced over to see if Kayne was watching us. Fortunately, he was outside of the garage with Damen, next to the Yukon.

"So can we hook up sometime when you ain't wit yo nigga?" By this time his hand was on my hip, and he moved another step closer.

Damn this nigga got heart, I thought to myself. "Na. We don't need to be hookin' up. Ain't no point," I answered blankly, pushing him away and walking over to Kayne. I kissed him on the lips to reassure Derrick that I was taken. He stood next to Damen giving Kayne an evil look. Of course Kayne didn't see this; he was busy talking with Damen.

"Come on Derrick, I'll take you back around to the lot so you can pick up your car and go home," Damen said getting in his car.

"A man, thanks for drivin' the car over here for us," Kayne said to Derrick.

"No problem," he replied. He looked at me one last time. I gave him a smile, as he and Damen drove off. I felt kind of bad for making him so salty, but I felt kind of proud too. Finally, I was able to resist somebody. I was making progress. I couldn't understand what made him want to get with me anyway, with my face all fucked up.

"What was that kiss for?" Kayne asked once we were alone.

"I can't give my nigga a kiss?" I smiled.

"Yeah. I just wasn't expectin' it. That's all."

"Next time I want a kiss. I'll tell you ahead of time."

"All that ain't necessary." He kissed me again.

"How long I gotta wait before I can get that?" He pulled me towards him, with his hands on my ass.

"Three weeks."

"Three weeks?"

"Yeah, I'm sorry." I didn't even know how I was going to wait three weeks.

"Na, don't be sorry. It ain't yo fault. You worth the wait anyway."

"I know." I hugged him.

"Get yo lil' conceded ass in da car."

"I'm hungry," I said as he drove off.

"What you want?"

"Chinese."

"You ain't pose to be eatin' nothin' but soup, you know that."

"Chinese ain't hard to chew; I'll just get some noodles."

"Aight, but that's it 'cause I ain't taking you back to no hospital 'cause you ain't do what the doctor told you. You want it to go?"

"Yeah, I'm tired," I said, leaning my seat back.

After stopping to get my food, we went back to his apartment located on Euclid in Corryville. Not too far from where Zelle's apartment was.

"How come you didn't tell me you was from Chicago?" I asked as we sat down to eat at the kitchen table.

"I don't know, you never asked," he simply replied. I just looked at him in silence. "What's that look for? You mad?"

"No. I just think it was something you shoulda brought up."

"Why?"

"I don't know, just forget I said anything." It was just like he did forget, because he didn't say anything else the whole time we ate. When I finished, I got up and ran some hot bath water. I relaxed my nerves in the tub for a whole hour. When I got out and walked into Kayne's room, he had candles lit all around the room. It was pretty romantic for him. I was somewhat confused on what he planned to do though, considering that we couldn't have sex.

"Take that towel off, and come lay down; I'ma give you a body massage." The way he looked at me had me wanting him like I had never wanted anybody before. I slowly dropped the towel revealing my bare body and laid on my stomach.

Kayne placed his hands on my shoulders and massaged them until he loosened my tenseness. Then he got a bottle of massage oil from the table next to the bed. As soon as he poured the oil onto my back I could smell the seducing aroma. He massaged from my back all the way down to my ankles, not missing a spot. By the time he was done, I felt like someone had given me a whole new body.

"Thank you, baby." I rolled over, kissing him on his sweet lips.

"Here put this on." He threw me a white T that was so big it nearly swallowed me up.

"It's big as hell."

"Lay back down so I can finish."

"What now?"

"Your feet." He grabbed my right foot, and began massaging it with the oil.

"You got some little feet, but they pretty. I thought you was gon' have bunions, and corns and shit," he laughed.

"Shut up, don't act like you ain't never seen my feet before." I closed my eyes and relaxed my head on the pillows propped behind me, as he continued to sooth me with his hands. When he was done he gave me clean boxers to put on, since I didn't have anything to sleep in.

"I'll give you some money to go shopping tomorrow while I help Damen pack his shit up over at the house."

"Ok." I got under the covers. Kayne blew out all the candles and left me in the room alone. He cracked the door just enough to hear his conversation when the phone rang, a few minutes later.

"Hello?" It was the first time I had heard him answer without saying yeah. There was a pause. "Who the fuck is this? Look, I ain't got time to be playin' no lil' guessing games wit hoes, who is this? Shit, I can't tell. You must be one. Callin' here askin' can you come suck my dick. I gotta girl I ain't on that shit." I wanted to pick up the phone next to the bed and go off on whoever he was talking to but I decided to listen some more.

"You lookin' for who?" he continued. "Zelle locked up, who is this Shanetta?...Aight, I ain't 'bout to keep playin' wit yo ass, bitch." He hung up.

I was so curious if it was Amber, and I figured that Shanetta was the girl that Zelle was with the night I got raped.

Kayne came in and sat down on the bed next to me. I had my eyes closed trying to forget about what I had just heard. He kissed me softly on the lips. I kept my eyes shut, but I could feel him sitting there watching me. He made me feel safe, and eventually I drifted off to sleep.

Chapter 14

Thursday - August 21, 2003

"Get up Baby." Kayne was shaking me trying to wake me up. The room still smelled like the vanilla scented candles he had burned the night before.

"Why?" I wined wishing he would let me go back to sleep.

"We need to leave in an hour. You know how long it takes you to get dressed."

"What time is it?"

"Nine."

"Kayne, it's too early."

"No it ain't. We tryna have everything ready to go by two."

"Ok." I dragged myself out of the bed to get some clothes from the bag that Zelle had brought to the hospital. I picked out a simple velour dress by Ecko Red that I hadn't worn yet.

"Here, Shayna is going shopping with you. So you ain't gotta drive." He handed me a thick wad of money. I counted it out. It was seven thousand.

"Thanks." We left at ten-thirty. Shayna was already at Damen's when we got there. I was so happy to see her. I needed to be around a female for a while after being with all·males for so long.

"Damen, we should be back around two," she said as we got ready to leave out.

"Ok, we should be done by then," he said.

"Bye," I said, kissing him.

"Be careful," he said.

"We just goin' shoppin', I'll be aight," I assured him.

"Yeah, we'll probably just go to Saks," Shayna chimed in.

"Aight." He let go of his grip. I hugged Damen and we left.

"I heard about what happened. I would have come to the hospital, but I was out of town visiting my sick mother in Atlanta," Shayna said as soon as we got in the car headed downtown to Saks.

"What's wrong with her?"

"She's got breast cancer."

"Aw, I'm sorry. How's she doin?"

"Actually, she's doing a lot better than she was. What about you?"

"I'm good. I don't have any kind of pain, just bleeding. The doctor says it should stop by Sunday."

"I know you hate that."

"It's not as bad as I thought it would be. It comes and goes, last night it stopped for a while."

"Well, that's good. Damen was a nervous wreck. He called

me as soon as he heard. But you look beautiful, like nothing ever happened."

"Thanks." I was being polite. I knew I looked better than when I first got to the hospital, but I didn't agree on the beautiful part.

"I know how you feel. I was raped when I was fifteen."

"For real?"

"Yeah, I started being fast when I was thirteen. Going out to parties, drinkin', smokin', everything I wasn't supposed to be doing. When I was fifteen, I got involved with a 25-year-old. I thought everything was ok until one night we were at his apartment, and he raped me. I wasn't a virgin, but I had told him that I didn't want to have sex and he just didn't wanna take no for an answer. After that I chilled out a little bit."

"Damn that's messed up. Were you living in Atlanta?"

"No. My mom moved out there a few years ago, I'm from here."

"So it happened here?"

"Yeah. I had it coming though. That's why you have to watch what you do and who you trust. Words don't mean shit no more, people lie to get whatever they want. I'm not trying to preach to you, because you're almost grown, but just remember that you're never too old to get raped or killed."

"You're right." Her words seemed to stick in my head like my mom's words about trust.

"And, you know you can call me up if you ever need to talk. I have to give you my number. We can chill, go shoppin' whatever. Just let me know. I don't do much besides go to work and visit Damen."

"Where you work at?"

"I'm an accountant at Provident in Hide Park. You know I live out there."

"Yeah, you told me. What you and Damen gon' do when he leaves? I mean you still gon' be together?"

"Of course. I'm thinking about moving to Chicago too, if I can find a job. I'm 35; it's about time I settle down. I don't know why he's running away from here anyway, but Damen is used to moving around a lot I guess."

"Yeah, I don't understand it either and you don't even look 35."

"Aww thanks," she laughed.

"How long have you been with Damen?"

"Since he moved here in 2001."

"You make a cute couple."

"You think so? I'm gonna miss him so much. I'll probably just up and move job or no job."

"You don't even have to work, living with Damen."

"Yeah, I really don't. But I guess I'm just used to working. How long have you and Kayne been together?"

"Exactly six days," I laughed.

"I think you two are cute together. I know at first Zelle did-n't like it at all. How's he doing anyway? Have you heard from him?"

"No, I haven't talked to him since he got locked up. I just hope he can get out."

"Me too. He doesn't need to be in jail. Damen will probably get his cousin Terrance to help him out. He's a judge here in Cincinnati. He kind of helps people out if they pay him."

"What is he some kind of dirty judge?" I laughed.

"Well, somethin' like that. He lived in Chicago with his mother, Damen's aunt, when he was younger. He was a drug dealer then. But he got out of that and moved up here with his sister who married somebody from Cincinnati. He really got himself together."

"You met him before?"

"Yeah. He's really nice. Nice looking too."

"Where does he live?"

"I think Mt. Adams."

"Wonder why I never met him."

"Damen and him don't really talk like that, just on occasion."

"Oh." We pulled up in front of Saks Fifth Avenue. It brought back memories of my first and only time shopping there with my first sugar daddy in 2001. He bought me a $2,000 Christian Dior dress to wear to his friend's club opening. I was the envy of the clique that night. Kelly and Trina had nothing on me in their $200 dresses. Their sugar daddy's weren't nearly as big time as mine.

Once inside the lavish department store, Shayna spotted a silk baby blue slip style Donna Karen dress with spaghetti straps and lace around the neckline and bottom.

"Girl ain't this cute?" She held it up to her.

"Yeah, it's my favorite color too." I was hoping she wasn't planning on buying it.

"Go try it on." She handed it to me, and continued looking on the rack.

"Ok." I walked into the dressing room.

There was a girl in the stall next to me, carrying on a conversation with another girl next to her. "Yeah. I told you I called him last night. He tried to act like he ain't know who I was. Talkin' bout he ain't into my lil' guessin' games. Whatever." The more I listened the more familiar the conversation sounded. It was Amber. I was so busy listening, I forgot all about trying on the dress. "I'm gonna get his ass just like I got Zelle. And I'ma get whoever shot Steelo," she continued. I wondered what she meant but I kept listening. I wanted all the information I could get so that when I beat her ass, I had all the reason in the world.

"Girl you need to, he think that money there to stay. He would be too shitty if he got knocked just like his boy did." *What the fuck? Who is that bitch?* I thought to myself. I would be sure to get a lick in on her too. I knew it was probably her sidekick Neesha.

"I still can't believe he gone," Amber sighed.

"Girl me either, ain't it a trip we in here spendin' Zelle's money. You ever think we would be shoppin' in Saks? We on some rich shit now," she laughed with satisfaction.

"I know, poor Zelle. Hope he don't drop the soap," she laughed obnoxiously.

"Yeah, your uncle came through. He went and picked his ass up instantly."

"I told you, he hates drug dealers. Every time one try to play me to the left I just tell him and they gone."

"And Zelle did try to play you like a hoe."

"Yeah, but he got what he deserved and Kayne is next. Girl guess who fuckin' wit him."

"Who?"

"That one light-skinned bitch from down the way, that always be wit that one lil'' hoe, Kelly. That's Zelle's sister," Amber said in a frustrated tone.

"Oh, the one that Steelo set up, I know who you talkin' 'bout. She dumb as hell. I will slide her young ass, believe that." Neesha laughed her annoying laugh again. Just then, I noticed Amber slipping on her shoes and heard her unlock the stall door.

"Come on let's go. I'ma just get this skirt." She stood in front of her friend's dressing room.

"I'm almost ready, hold on," she said.

I left my dressing room and walked up behind Amber. I guess she felt me behind her because she turned around with a startled look on her face. When she realized it was me she tried to move away, but I caught her in the jaw as hard as I could. When her friend heard her head slam against the door she rushed out.

"What the fuck?!" Neesha yelled pulling my hair.

"I knew it was yo corny ass. Bitch you a slide me?" I said catching Neesha with one to the face too. Then I pushed her into the full-length mirror inside her dressing room, and got back to beating Amber's ass who was trying to jump on my back.

The glass cracked and fell on Neesha's back causing her to fall to the ground.

"Amina?…" I heard Shayna calling, but I continued to fight Amber.

I pushed her off of my back. We both fell to the floor. I was on my knees punching her over and over until I saw blood running out of her nose. She tried to put me in a headlock, but she failed.

"What are you doin' Amina? Girl you pregnant!" Shayna yelled running into the dressing room. She dropped the clothes in her hand and pulled me up off of Amber who was scratching my face. When Amber got back up I broke away from Shayna and hit her with an uppercut causing her to stumble to the floor. I slammed her head into the wall about six times.

"Amina! Stop!" Shayna screamed.

As I turned to face Shayna, Amber pulled a box cutter from inside her jean pocket and jammed it directly in the middle of my stomach. I fell to the floor and let out a loud scream of pain. Shayna caught Amber with two punches in a row that knocked her back to the floor. Amber crawled over to Neesha, they both helped each other up then ran out past the two store workers who were approaching. Shayna knelt down next to me and gently pulled the box cutter from my stomach.

"What happened?" The store workers both screamed looking down at me and the pool of blood that was soaking into the white carpet.

"What does it look like? She just got stabbed! Call the fuckin' ambulance!" Startled, they both ran to the phone. "It's ok. Just hold on. Ok?" Shayna said covering the wound that was still squirting blood with a skirt she had brought in to try on. I didn't even nod and before I knew it I had blacked out.

When I did finally wake back up, I was in a hospital bed, again, with Kayne sitting next to me and Shayna standing over me.

"Hey," she whispered, giving a half smile.

"Did I lose it?! Did I lose my baby?!" I cried loudly.

"Ssshhh. We don't know yet," Kayne said grabbing my hand, trying to calm me. Just as I was about to go crazy, Damen walked in.

"There's my princess," he smiled. "Hey sleeping beauty, you're up now. I missed those pretty eyes." He kissed me on the cheek. I cried some more, but harder this time. Kayne sat there shaking his head. He looked mad. The doctor came in, and my crying ceased.

"Amina? I'm afraid we have bad news," he said. It was a different doctor than before. I guessed that I was in a different hospital, but I didn't know. I didn't even bother to ask what the news was because I already knew.

"She lost it?" Shayna asked.

"Yes, I'm sorry. Amina suffered a miscarriage before we even got her into the emergency room. I'm sorry you were kept waiting for the news."

The room was silent, the doctor walked out. Kayne went behind him. My crying started again. Damen held my hand for a while. "I'm gonna go get Kayne," he walked out too.

Shayna hugged me. "It's alright, go ahead and cry," she said. I sat up to dry my eyes with the tissue she handed me.

"Shayna, I'm so tired of crying. I don't wanna cry no more." Tears still fell from my eyes.

"I know sweetie, but you gotta let it out. It's alright to cry."

"I don't have nobody no more. Damen's leaving, Zelle's gone, and I don't even have a mom no more."

"No...don't say that. Damen's still gonna be there, he'll just be living in Chicago. You can always talk to him, and you've got me and Kayne and your friends Trina and Kelly. Just because you and your mom fell out doesn't mean she's not your mother anymore she'll always be your mom."

"I fell out with Kelly too, I don't want to talk to her or Trina and my momma don't care about me. She ain't even pick up the phone and call."

"I'll drive you to see her as soon as you get out of here. I'm sure she'll be happy to see you. Sometimes you have to take the first step, or it'll never happen."

I knew she was right, and I hoped she would be happy to see me because no matter how much I denied it, I needed her. "Ok, maybe you're right," I told her.

"Damen said he won't leave until you're back home and settled."

"When do I leave?"

"The doctors told us Wednesday."

"Isn't it Thursday?"

"No baby, it's Friday morning, 10:15 a.m."

"Oh." I laid my head back on the pillow. I still felt sleepy.

"Zelle gets visitor hours on Friday. Kayne's taking you to see him."

"Has Damen called his cousin, Terrance?"

"No, he's been so worried about you."

"Does Zelle know...about me?"

"Yeah. He called Damen's house yesterday right before him and Kayne left out to come to the hospital. Kayne said he flipped when Damen told him."

"He probably did."

"So, how you feelin'?"

"Like shit. I can't believe it's gone. I wanted my baby."

"I know, but you can't fight while you're pregnant Mina. You know that."

"Yeah, but Amber was the reason Zelle got locked up. I heard their whole conversation. She was telling her friend that she had him arrested by her uncle because he played her for a hoe, and that Kayne was next."

"Oh my goodness!" Shayna's jaw dropped.

"I know fighting her was stupid, I just let my anger get the best of me."

"You can't feed into everything. She might be the reason Zelle is locked up but she's also the reason you lost your baby." She was completely right. Amber would be satisfied when she heard that she killed my baby, and she was probably still planning to snitch on Kayne. Damen and Kayne walked back into the room.

"I'm sorry for walkin' out like that. I had to chill out for a minute. I'm tired of seein' you goin' through all this bullshit, you don't deserve it. But I ain't gon' let nothin' else happen I promise." He kissed me. "Shayna tell you I'm takin' you to see Zelle next Friday?"

"Yeah, she takin' me to see my mom too."

"When Friday?"

"Thursday."

"I'ma go wit you, cause if anything else happen I'ma kill somebody."

"Ok."

"Mina, I'm about to leave. I gotta be at work in an hour. I'll be here tomorrow around twelve," Shayna said, giving me a hug and kiss on the cheek.

"And I'm supposed to be meeting these people that's comin' to pick up these cars," Damen said doing the same. "I love you."

"I love you too."

After they both left, I told Kayne about Amber setting Zelle up. He told me not to worry about it, that we would take care of it later and to just go to sleep. So I did. When I opened my eyes again, Brell and Swag were in the room.

"What up lil' nigga?" Brell greeted me with his devilish grin that I always thought was cute even when were in grade school.

"Hi, what yaw doin' here?"

"What you mean, we ain't forgot 'bout you," Swag said.

"How'd you know what happened?"

"I heard through Freddy, you know Amber told him every-thing like she did you or somethin' but we all know you beat her ass. If you didn't, she wouldn't of had to stab you."

"Yeah. I beat her ass and Neesha ass too. And wait till I get out."

"You don't need to do shit else. I'll tell Kelly to take care of it. She already lookin' for Amber," Brell said.

"I don't talk to her big mouth ass no more, and you can tell her I don't need her help."

"Come on now man, yaw go all the way back to fifth grade and you just gon' stop talkin' just like that? What she say?" Swag said.

"She just gotta big mouth period; every little thing I tell her between me and her gets spread around in less than an hour. She just love drama and I ain't fuckin' wit her no more."

"Yeah, you say that now but yaw gon' be right back togeth-er when you get out." Brell downplayed my anger.

"Whatever, think what you want," I said rolling my eyes.

"Kelly was the one that called to find out what hospital you was in. We asked her to come, but she ain't want to. She said she knew you was mad, and Trina in Florida with her momma. You still talk to her right?"

"Yeah. Where's Kayne?" I asked trying to switch the subject.

"He went to get some food," Brell answered.

"Oh, I am kinda hungry," I said. The room fell quiet, Kayne walked in with three bags. He handed Brell and Swag their own separate bags and gave them each their change. I guessed they had already introduced themselves to him.

"Here you go baby." He took my food out of the bag and put it on the tray for me.

"Can I eat this?" I asked looking at the hamburger and fries in front of me.

"Yeah, you can eat it. I wouldn't go buy you no shit you can't eat. What you think, I'm tryna kill you?"

"I hope not." I answered eating two fries.

"You know me better than that." He began eating too.

After Brell and Swag left, Kayne and I sat up all night until about 3 a.m. watching movies and videos. He never left my side. Most niggas wouldn't be bothered with a female, who stayed in so much shit. I made up my mind that now, I trusted him.

Triple Crown Publications presents

Chapter 15

Thursday - August 28, 2004

Shayna came by Kayne's at three o'clock, to pick me up to go see my mom, but I decided to drive instead. It had been a while since I had driven my Lexus. Kayne and Shayna were ok with it, they seemed happy to see me back to normal.

Shayna sat in the back seat and Kayne took shotgun on the ride downtown. When we got to my mom's apartment, Kayne and Shayna stayed in the car while I went to knock on the door. I felt it was something I needed to do alone. I would tell them to get out if she was home. I didn't call first because I didn't want to give her the chance to turn me away. I wanted to talk face to face.

Before I even went up the steps, I started to get nervous, but I continued anyway. I knocked on the door twice. I hoped that Markus wouldn't be the one who answered. I knocked again, two more times.

"I'm coming!" Someone yelled. It was a woman's voice, but it didn't sound anything like my mom. "Hello?" The women said when she finally opened the door. She was a short, fat white woman with long brown hair and an orange tan. She looked about 45 and spoke with a southern accent.

What the hell is she doing living in my momma's house? I thought to myself. "Is Kayla here?" I asked wishing she would say yes, even though I knew it wasn't likely.

"Who?" Her eyebrow rose up.

"Kayla Moore, black lady, short, brown skinned, long jet black hair?"

"Oh, naw. She moved out 'bout a week ago."

"You know where she went?" I asked disappointed, and desperate for more information on the whereabouts of my mom.

"I don't know. She moved out with some man. People in the building say they was happy to see them two go. They used to be up all hours of the night fightin'. They say he used to beat the livin' mess outta that women. I don't know where they moved to, but it's somewhere out of state...I do know that."

I couldn't believe what she was telling me. Markus had been beating my mom and she still hadn't got the sense to leave him. I wondered if she ever even tried. Either way it didn't matter. I would probably never see her again; Markus would probably kill her one day.

"Ok, thank you." I walked down the steps about ready to cry. By the time I got into the car tears had filled my eyes. I was surprised I even had any tears left after all the shit I had been through in the past few weeks.

"What's happened?" Kayne asked.

"She gone."

"What?" Shayna asked scooting closer from the backseat.

"The lady that lives there said she and Markus moved a week ago, and she said that people in the building said he used to beat her all the time. They moved somewhere out of town."

"She don't know where?" Kayne asked.

"No."

"Well, why don't we go ask some other people in the building, maybe they know where she moved," Shayna suggested.

"Maybe my grandma does." With a little hope, I dialed her number.

"Hello?" she answered

"Hi, Grandma."

"Mimi?"

"Yeah, it's me Grandma."

"Aww baby, why you just now callin? I been so worried about you. I heard what happened. Where you stayin' at now?"

"With my brother." I lied I couldn't afford to tell her the truth or everything that had went on because she would make sure I came to live with her.

"Where's that at?"

"Corryville. Have you heard from my mom?"

"She came by one time right before she left last Thursday, lookin' terrible—black eye, busted lip and everything. I tried to stop her from going to Texas with that crazy man, but your momma's always been hard headed. She'll learn."

"Where in Texas?"

"I don't know it was some small town his people stay in. I can't even remember the name, but when I do I'll give you a call. What's the number over there?"

"Oh, grandma I gotta go this phone is going dead. I'll call you back later and give you the number," I lied.

"Ok, baby. Make sure you do that. Love you."

"I love you too." I hung up.

"What she say?" Shayna asked.

"They moved to some small town in Texas, she can't remember the name."

"I'm so sorry Mina." Shayna rested her head on my shoulder.

"Yeah, let's just go. Kayne, can you please drive home?"

"Yeah."

We all rode back in silence; I didn't have to tell them, they knew I didn't want to talk about the situation anymore. When we got home, I laid in the bed staring off into space. Shayna sat beside me trying to get me to talk, but I wouldn't. Finally, she left around seven.

Damen came almost as soon as she left. He tried getting me to talk too, but nothing would work. I felt no need for words. He was leaving to go back to Chicago the next morning.

"Here Mina, this is a gift I brought for you. Open it whenever you get ready, but make sure you open the gift first. I may be leaving, but I want you to remember that I love you. I don't want you to think I'm walking out again. If you want to come with me, it's not too late to say so." He looked at me waiting for a response, but my eyes kept straight ahead and my lips didn't move. "Ok," he said with disappointment, sitting the gift box and card down. Then he kissed me lightly on the cheek. I still didn't look at him. "I'll call you as soon as I get to Chicago." He left out and closed the door behind him. I glanced over at the gift box; it was small and wrapped in gold paper with a black bow. I didn't feel like opening it, I didn't even care what was inside. It could never replace Damen, and definitely would never replace Zelle, or my mom, or the baby I'd lost. As far as I was concerned, it wasn't important.

Chapter 16

Friday - August 29, 2003

Kayne tried to get me to eat last night, but I wouldn't. I never went to sleep either. When he turned out the lights to go to sleep, I stayed up with my eyes open until sunrise. He woke up at ten and I was still laying there, eyes wide open. I could have been mistaken for dead. I was hoping he wasn't planning on going anywhere soon, because I just wanted to lie there at least for another hour.

"Baby, you hungry? I was gon' fix breakfast," he asked, trying to get me to eat once again. I shook my head to say no. "Come on Mina, you gotta eat somethin'. You ain't ate since yesterday mornin'." I didn't respond. "Can you please say something?" I was silent. "Baby please," he begged. I stayed silent. "Will you talk when we go see Zelle?" I nodded yes.

We got to the Justice Center at 1:30 p.m.; we waited in line for a whole thirty minutes. The majority of the line was made up of women, some young, some middle-aged. They all were either pregnant or had at least one kid with them, and I hated them all for it.

We were eventually called in to see Zelle. Kayne sat down and picked up the phone first, he told Zelle about the situation with my mother and how I didn't talk for almost two days. Then he told him about Amber, I stood behind him as they talked. Zelle looked at me with a look I had never seen on his face before. He looked me in the eyes like he could feel every bit of my pain. Maybe he could.

When Kayne saw us make eye contact, he got up and handed me the phone. I sat down.

"Hey baby girl, I miss you," Zelle smiled.

"I miss you too. A lot." It had been so long since I heard my voice I almost forgot I had one, and it seemed like a decade since I had heard Zelle's voice.

"It's a mothafucka in here, but it ain't shit compared to what's been goin' on with you back home. How you holdin' up?"

"I'm aight, I just need you to come back home," I told him.

"I wish I could, but it won't be long. I'ma get outta here don't worry bout me, It's you I'm worried about."

"I'm ok."

"No you ain't. I can see it in yo eyes." He was right, I wasn't ok. I looked down so he couldn't see my eyes anymore.

"I'm fine, Zelle."

"How Kayne treatin' you?"

"Like a queen," I said looking up smiling, and reminding him of when he told me Kayne wouldn't treat me like a queen. He gave me a half-smile.

"Guess I was wrong, huh?"

"Yeah. But it's ok, you was just tryin' to protect me."

"Glad you finally realized that. I got somebody for Amber."

"For real? Who?"

"This chic from Chicago named Shadow. If you pay her enough she'll fly out here and take care of her ass in a day." This girl Shadow sounded kind of crazy, but I wanted to get Amber so bad I would have paid her any amount to get rid of her.

"You got her number?"

"Kayne'll give it to you. But you have to meet up with her, she don't really like Kayne."

"Why not?" I asked defensively.

"It ain't that she don't like him, she just got salty at him 'cause he wouldn't fuck with her. She crazy, but she'll get the job done."

"Oh, aight."

"Anyway, that was some years ago. I don't know what's up now. I still want you to be the one to call."

"Ok, I will. When was the last time you talked to her?"

"'Bout a month ago."

"Is Kayne giving me the money?"

"Yeah. Where else you gon get it from?"

"Oh."

"I'ma send you a letta on yo birthday."

"Ok. I'll be checkin' the mail."

He looked at the clock on the wall. "Aight make sho you don't let Shadow know where you stay. Meet her somewhere, and only give her yo cell number."

"I got it." The guard showed up behind Zelle.

"Times up Costello," he said dryly.

"Mina, I love you. And hey, don't you and Kayne move too fast," he said looking serious.

"I love you too." We both hung up. The time I had with Zelle was short, but I would have been grateful for sixty seconds just to say I love you.

When we got home I called Shadow from my cell right away. Kayne gave me the number, and then he went out to pick up some food. I was ready to get Amber out of the picture so that I could finally relax.

The person that answered the phone whispered hello, as if they had no voice.

"Is this Shadow?" I asked. I couldn't tell if it was a male or female.

"Yes, who is this?" she continued to whisper.

"My name is Amina, I'm Zelle's sister. You know him right?"

"Oh, for real? You Zelle's lil people's?"

"Un-huh."

"How old are you?"

"I'll be eighteen November 7th."

"Where you stay?"

"In Cincinnati."

"What you need?"

"I got somebody I want you to take care of for me. Her name is Amber."

"Aight, but can I ask why?"

"She got Zelle locked up, and she stabbed me." It took everything I had not to let Shadow hear my sadness.

"Zelle's in jail? Oh my God, when this happen?"

"Last week."

"Damn, that's fucked up. How long he get?"

"We don't really know for sure yet, but I think we lookin' at about ten years."

"So how did ol' girl manage this?"

"Her uncle is 5-0; I guess she just told him to arrest him. She claim Zelle played her for a hoe, but I don't know how, and I really don't care I just want her dead."

"Shit, I do too. So she lives in Cincinnati too?"

"No, she stay in Covington, Kentucky; right across the bridge."

"Ok. That sounds pretty easy. When you tryin' to have this done?"

"ASAP."

"I'll fly into Cincinnati Sunday afternoon. What's your address?"

"I'll meet you downtown at the Four Points Sheraton, at the bar in the lobby."

"Where's that?"

"Fifth street."

"Ok. So is this the number I should call when I get there."

"Yeah."

"Ok. I'll call you to let you know when my flight will be

landing, and as soon as I get in town. Then we can meet up and discuss the details."

"Alright." We both hung up.

Sunday – August 31, 2003

Shadow was right on schedule. She called me Sunday at around three. She had already checked into a room at the Four Points, and told me to meet her there at nine. It had taken me since Friday night to talk Kayne into letting me go alone. He told me he didn't care if Shadow liked him or not. But I assured him that things would be ok. We would be in a public place. He agreed and gave me five stacks that morning.

"It shouldn't cost more than this," he told me.

At eight o' clock, I got dressed. I wore some fitted black dress pants and a white tailored shirt that I had buttoned low, showing my huge cleavage in my black lace bra, with all black stilettos. I had picked all of this up on my shopping spree Saturday afternoon. When I was completely dressed, I decided to open the gift from Damen. I opened the present before just like he told me to. I would have done it that like that anyway, it was a habit.

In the nicely wrapped gift box was a Diamond necklace with a diamond crown charm. I put it on and opened the card. A small piece of paper fell out; it had Terrance's number written on it. I began to read the hand-written card.

Amina,

I know this is a couple of months early but considering my current situation I wanted you to have it before shit got worst. It's a birthday present for you. I gave you the crown charm because you're my princess, and you will always be my princess. I want you to know that even though I'm in Chicago, I'm always here for you whenever you need me. You've been through a lot lately, too much actually. But remember storms always pass.

*The number I gave you is Terrance Savellman, your cousin.
He's a judge down at the courthouse on Main. He'll get Zelle
out within a year. I've already talked to him; he's expecting
your phone call. He wants to be in touch with you about Zelle
since you're right there in Cincinnati. He lives in Mt. Adams.
You don't have to meet him just give him a call sometime to
see what's going on. I'll be keeping in touch with him too. And
please don't forget to be careful in everything you do.*

Love,

Daddy

I was thankful for the gift. I finally had something that I could keep forever from Damen. He was right when he said that storms always pass, my storm seemed to be passing over a little already, although not completely.

"Damn, I thought you was going to see Shadow," Kayne said when I walked into the living room where he was sitting.

"I am."

"You look like you goin' to meet a nigga."

"What you mean? I always dress like this."

He gave me a cold stare. "No, you don't."

"Yes, I do," I argued.

"Aight, whatever Mina. Bye."

"Don't tell me bye like that," I snapped. He gave me another blank stare. "You wanna come with me and see ain't shit goin' on?"

"No, I didn't say it was. I said what you look like you was doin'."

Annoyed, I looked at my watch. It was 8:35 p.m. I hated getting my knees dirty while I was looking so good, but I wanted to loosen the tension between Kayne and me. I slipped off my shoes, and grabbed a pillow from the couch to kneel on.

I unzipped his jeans and pulled his dick out. It was bigger than Maurice and Steelo. I worked my magic giving him the best head job he would ever get, and had him cumming in less than five minutes. I could feel his body loosen up. I put my shoes back on and went to wash out my mouth. When I looked at Kayne he looked like a totally different person.

"Bye baby, I should be back by 11 at the latest." I kissed him and walked out.

I made it to the hotel by 8:50 p.m. I tipped the valet and went inside to the bar. As soon as I sat down heads were turning. Three men sitting together at a table looked my way, but I ignored them. I ordered a Long Island Ice tea using my fake I.D., of course.

As I sipped my drink, I looked around for Shadow. She had described herself as light-skinned, tall and thick with long brown hair. I checked my watch, it was 9:10. When I looked up there was a woman approaching where I was sitting. It was her; she looked exactly how she had described herself. She wore a plain red long sleeved shirt, tucked into dark denim jeans with simple black slide-ins, and her hair was pulled into a ponytail. She looked like she was on her way to the grocery store, while I on the other hand, looked like I was on a hot date. Still, I didn't feel uncomfortable, looking good was an everyday thing for me.

"Are you Amina?" She asked sitting down on the stool next to me.

"Yeah, and you're Shadow right?"

"Yep," she smiled. She was a lot prettier than I expected. "So, I'm guessing you brought a fake I.D." She looked at my drink.

"Yeah. I always keep that," I said taking a sip.

"That's smart. But you probably could have did without one you look about 21."

"Can I buy you a drink?"

"Yeah, thanks. I'll take a brandy," she said. I caught the attention of the bartender, who was looking at a football game.

"Well, let's get down to business," I said after she was served.

"Ok, first I need to know where she lives."

"In Covington on Scott Street. I don't know the exact address." I went on to tell her all the information Kayne had gotten from Zelle.

"Ok that means I'll have to watch her a while. What's the color of her house?"

"It's a red brick house, but what is a while?"

"Ok I'll ask around." Shadow ignored my question.

"Wait don't you think that will make it obvious?"

"Look, I've done this at least seventeen times and my slate is clean. I'm not even in the system. Just trust me. Besides, I only ask around as a last resort; I mean if watching the house doesn't work."

"Ok." I took a deep breath.

"Now, what does she look like?"

"A little shorter than me, goldish hair cut short, brown skin, and real small lips. Oh and she's got a mole on her right cheek."

Shadow took note while I spoke. "How old is she?"

"Nineteen or twenty."

"You don't know her last name?"

"No."

"Ok, now we can talk about how you want it done. It's completely up to you, but I use knives, guns, and poison. I know you're probably thinking poison? That sounds like some old snow white type shit, but to me that's the best way. It's quick, and best of all… no blood."

"How much will that run me?"

"Since you're Zelle's peoples, I'll do it for four stacks but I usually charge six. I have to split the money with my partner."

"Who's your partner?"

"His name is Pitt. He's driving down here; he should be here in the morning."

"Ok, so what's the plan?"

"Well, I'll have Pitt set her up to come to the hotel then we can plant the poison in her drink and it's done."

"How you know that he can get Amber?"

"Pitt's a pro just like me. He's driving his Jaguar down here. I'm pretty sure she won't turn that down. But correct me if I'm wrong, you're the one that knows her."

"Right," I admitted.

"But what does he look like? How old is he?"

"Pitt is twenty-two and he's real sexy—tall, dark-skinned, pretty smile, and pretty teeth."

"Alright." I trusted her judgment.

"So like I said, I'll sit on the street in my rental, then when I spot her that's where Pitt comes in."

"Don't you think it's kind of risky right here in a hotel?"

"No. I've done it plenty of times."

"What you gon' do with the body? How will you get it out of here?" I asked, it didn't sound logical.

"Look, let's just do it a little easier. Forget the poison, we'll do stabbing instead. Pitt can drive her to an isolated place. We'll keep her body in the trunk until we find a good place for it. Does that sound better?"

"Ok, but where will he drive her?"

"Pitt will find a place he doesn't even have to know the area."

"You sure?"

"Yes. I'm sure."

"Will the price change?"

"No."

"Can't yaw just do a drive by or some shit like that?"

"If that's how you want it done, you can do that yourself why would you pay me? I don't do things that way I'm classy with my work," she said sounding insulted.

"Ok, well I want the second plan."

"Alright. It's done then. I'll call as soon as I spot her, and keep you up to date from there on out."

"You still got my number right?"

"Yeah."

"Ok."

"And remember this is between me, you and Pitt."

"Oh, yeah I know." I paid for the drinks and got up to leave.

Triple Crown Publications presents

Chapter 17

Monday - November 6, 2003

It had been two months and two days since Amber was killed. Everything had gone perfectly. Shadow and Pitt had taken care of everything in exactly four days. I met up with Shadow and paid her on September 5th, one day after the actual murder. I never did see Pitt.

When I heard about Amber on the channel 9 news, I smiled with satisfaction. Covington Police were supposedly setting up an investigation, but it would be pointless since Shadow and Pitt were long gone.

It was the day before my birthday and me and Kayne were leaving for Puerto Rico in the morning. I was already packed and ready to go. Kayne had bought me a brand new Louis Vuitton luggage set, and taken me shopping for a swim suit. I got a Burberry and Chanel bathing suit with matching sunglasses for each.

Around nine o'clock at night, somebody was at the door.

"Who is it?" I asked with my hand on the doorknob.

"It's Shayna. Open up, these boxes are getting heavy." I opened the door; she was standing there with two nicely wrapped boxes.

"Hi, what's all this?" I said, already knowing it was for me.

"Gifts, for the birthday girl," she smiled.

I closed the door behind her and we both sat on the couch. "Awww, how sweet."

"Open the small box first."

"Ok." I unwrapped the gift box. Inside was an all white J.Lo velour catsuit.

"This is cute!" I said excitedly. I really did like it.

"You like it?"

"Yeah, this is hot. Thank you."

"You welcome. Next box," she directed. In the next box was a pair of all white Gucci boots. They were ankle high with a pencil heel. I loved them.

"Thank you, Shayna," I said sincerely giving her a hug.

"Aw, girl you welcome. You all ready for your big trip tomorrow?"

"Yeah, I'm all packed, so is Kayne; he's sleep right now. Our plane leaves tomorrow at 12:30."

"Yaw getting up early then."

"Yeah."

"You talked to Zelle?"

"Last week. I talked to Terrance too. He said he's tryin' his best to pull some strings."

"That's good, hopefully he comes through."

"Hopefully."

"What you gon' do when you get back? Are you still going to school?"

"Yeah." She gave me an unsure look. "I am, for real. Kayne makes me go everyday. Sometimes he drops me off and picks me up, but I usually drive," I told her.

"Good. Because you need to go ahead and graduate so you won't have to worry about it anymore."

"I know."

"You thought about getting a job?"

"No. I got everything I need and more with Kayne. He says I don't have to work, and Damen sends me money every month."

"Yeah, I know everything sounds good right now but you always need to be prepared for the worse, I mean you've basically already seen it. Even if you don't get a job, just get an account and save some money, so you have something to fall back on."

"You're right. I'll open one when I get back."

"Ok, you know you can always come to my bank and open up one." I nodded my head in agreement. Shayna could tell I was getting uncomfortable with where the conversation was going. "Well, let me go so you can get some rest for tomorrow. Have fun and be safe." She gave me a hug and got up to walk towards the door.

"I'll call you as soon as we get back."

"Ok, make sure you do," she smiled closing the door behind her.

Tuesday – November 7, 2003

We got to the airport thirty minutes before our plane was scheduled to depart. It took a whole twenty minutes just to get through the tight security. The lines were crazy. But fortunately, we made it to our plane on time. We stopped in Orlando to switch planes. The whole plane ride was relaxing to me, I never feared flying unlike my mom.

Once we touched down in Puerto Rico, I was expecting a cab to be waiting for us, but instead there was a white stretch limo. The chauffeur helped with our bags then helped me into the car where Kayne sat directly across from me. He opened a bottle of Belvedere, and poured us both a glass.

"Let's make a toast," he said. I lifted my glass. "To my baby on her birthday, I love you," he said clinging glasses with me. I was so caught up in the moment it took me a while to comprehend what he said. When it finally clicked, I had to ask to make sure I heard right.

"You love me?"

"Yeah, I love you. If I didn't I wouldn't be doing all this. It'll be three months on the 16th; it's something about you that's different from other females. I never even thought about bein' serious with nobody before, I never even been faithful to nobody until now." I could tell by his eyes that he was serious.

"I love you too," I said, honestly meaning it. I had been feeling the same way for a while; I just didn't know how to say it. We finished our drinks, then he kissed me and we didn't stop until the limo pulled into the Wyndham Hotel and casino in Old San Juan. I was ready to get to our room, because I knew what was coming up next. We both had been waiting a long time for it.

The hotel was fabulous, I loved the room. It was like nothing I had ever seen.

"You like it?" Kayne asked when we were settled in our room.

"Yeah, I love it." I walked over to look out of the window. It was a perfect view of the old Spanish town.

"Good. We can go to the beach tomorrow after I rent the car."

"Ok." I said gazing at the night sky. He walked up behind me and pulled me over to the bed. As I laid down, he began kissing me again. Starting with my lips he went to my neck, sucking until I could feel a mark appear. From there he gently lifted my shirt over my head, unsnapped my bra and took my already hard nipples in his mouth one by one, sucking softly making every juice in my body flow. After peeling my jeans off, his tongue found its final destination. He gently licked the inside of my pussy, teasingly biting and sucking on my clit, until my body went over the top with pleasure. He licked all of my juices that were rushing towards his face. I couldn't believe how good it felt. I knew this had to be his way of saying he really loved me.

When he was finished, I took position over him letting him know it was his turn. He laid back on the bed, and I took him in my mouth, like I'd been doing for the past three months. I worked my tongue exactly how I knew he liked me to. As I pleased him, he pleased me by using two fingers to loosen me up. After he decided he'd had enough foreplay, we switched positions again and he immediately found his way inside of me. The deeper he went, the louder my moans became. The sound of me saying his name in his ear only turned him on more and more. I loved it. We went on and on, over and over the whole night until both of our bodies were drained.

When the sun rose, Kayne was sleep, but I was still awake with his arms wrapped tightly around me. I felt safer than I ever had before. I didn't go to sleep because I didn't want to let go of that feeling. All the nights he had held me this way as we slept, and yet this night felt so different. I felt like I needed to hold onto it forever, like maybe it would be one of the last.

Saturday – November 11, 2003

We made our way down to the casino where I lost three hundred dollars, and Kayne came up on five hundred. I seemed to have absolutely no luck in any game that night. But nothing was bad enough to ruin my vacation, after all, it was the first and best one I would ever have.

Wednesday – November 15, 2003

Kayne took me shopping. I bought a cute little dress for Shayna, a couple of things for me, and a souvenir for Damen. The rest of the afternoon was spent lying on the beach drinking daiquiris with Kayne.

The paradise was interrupted by a phone call on Kayne's cell phone.

"Hello?" he answered. "What? When?" he asked the voice on the other end.

What now? I thought to myself as he continued his conversation.

"Yeah, I'm coming back Monday morning."

"Aight." He hung up. The look on his face was stressful.

I sat up in the lawn chair. "What happened?"

"My mans just told me there's a big drug bust going down right now. A lot of niggas got knocked. He said Feds been ridin' around my way askin' for me and shit."

"What?" My mind was a huge blur. All I could think about was what would happen when we got home.

"You ready to go back to the room?" Kayne was hiding his anger very well.

"Yeah," I answered still in shock. We drove back to the hotel in our rented black Nissan Maxima.

When we got back to the room, Kayne sat down at the desk and started writing on a pad of paper. I wondered what it said as

I laid on the bed watching him. I couldn't believe how calm he was. I knew he just didn't want to ruin the trip. When he was done he ripped the paper off and came to sit next to me. "I want you to just enjoy the rest of this trip. Don't let this shit stop you." I looked at him blankly, saying nothing. "You hear what I said?" He looked dead in my eyes.

"Yeah, I heard you. But what we gon' do?" I asked with worry.

"We?" he asked, seeming surprised.

"Hell yeah, we. *We* still together right?"

"Yeah."

"Well then, whatever trouble you in, I'm in." I really meant what I was saying. "What?" I asked when he didn't do anything but stare at me with a grin.

"Here." He handed me the piece of paper.

"What's this?" I asked reading it over, there were four names and numbers listed; two were out of town numbers. The last name was Terrance Savellman.

"A list of people who I trust that can help you come up with some money to get me out if I get locked up," he answered. "Booskey," he pointed at the name on the top of the list, "that's my nigga. If it ever come down to you having to use that list, go to him first," he instructed. "Savellman, he comes last," he continued.

"Why?" I asked confused.

"Savellman got his ways, and everything is supposed to be his way. I used to work for him back in the day when he lived in Chicago. He taught me and Zelle everything we know. He even taught Damen a lot about the game. He was good to me, started me off with somethin' when I needed it and I appreciate it. But I always remembered him leavin' niggas stuck when they got caught. He was always selfish, and probably still is."

147

"Nobody ever snitched on him?" I asked.

"Na, nobody was that crazy. T.S. had niggas pissin' in they pants just thinkin' bout what would happen if they said his name to the Feds."

"So you sayin' you don't think he would help you out?"

"He might, I don't know. But you see his name's the last on that list."

"He's helping Zelle, why don't you think he'll help you?"

"Zelle got privilege with him 'cause they related. It's different with me. Everything he ever did for me was in favor of Zelle because he knew we was close. We grown now and that shit is old."

"How long did you work for him?"

"I started when I was fourteen and he moved to Cincinnati when I was fifteen."

"Oh, what made him wanna become a judge?"

"He was already in law school in Chicago and hustled on the side. When his momma died, it made him want to get his life together. His mama was yo grandaddy's sister."

"Oh, ok." I was surprised at how much he knew about my family, it made me feel even more comfortable with him. "But, I still think he would be some help. can call and talk to him, and it would be good to tell him ahead of time," I suggested.

He gave me a hard stare. "Put that up, and don't lose it," he said pointing to the paper in my hand. The tone in his voice gave me the idea that he was pissed.

I got up to put it in my purse, and he got up to get in the shower. He stayed in there for what seemed like forever. By the time he came out, I had gotten undressed and went to sleep. The next morning I didn't wake up until 10 a.m., and Kayne wasn't there. I took a quick shower and got dressed to go look for Kayne and get some breakfast.

As soon as I got downstairs, I went to the window where I could see the parking lot. I didn't see our Maxima. I didn't understand where he could have gone. For a minute the idea of him leaving me stranded in Puerto Rico crossed my mind. But his things were still in the room, so I scratched that idea.

Ok, maybe he just went for a drive and didn't want to wake me up, I thought to myself as I made my way to the restaurant, and helped myself to the breakfast bar. I piled my plate with all kinds of things I knew I probably wouldn't even eat. I sat down at a table alone and began indulging in it.

"Is it good?" Kayne whispered in my ear startling me.

"You scared the shit out of me," I said dropping my fork.

"Where you been?" I was about to go off on him for leaving without telling me, but as soon as he sat down and looked me in my eyes giving me a sexy grin, I changed my mind. He pulled a small ring box out of his pocket.

My eyes got big as he opened it displaying a six carat diamond ring.

"What's this for?" I asked excitedly.

"It's a promise ring. I don't know what's gon' happen when I get home. The Feds prolly waitin' on my ass right now. Ain't no use in runnin' cause money gon' run out eventually. The money at the crib, I might as well say that's gone down the drain cause as soon as they raid my apartment they gon' get my shit. Amina, this ring is for you, so you don't forget who you belong to, who yo nigga is, and who love you. Once we leave this lil' paradise Monday, it's back to the grind. You say you down, but I need to know if you really mean it. If you really willin' to put in work for a nigga."

"I said I was. I'll do anything you need me to," I said as he slid the ring on my right ring finger.

"We'll see," he said getting up to go to the breakfast buffet.

"Where's your mom? She live in Chicago?" I asked after he sat back down. He looked at me like he was surprised by my question. "When I turned eighteen, she moved to L.A. with my grandma."

"Why?" I asked wishing I hadn't right after it came out. His whole expression changed, he seemed to have pain in his eyes.

"She had a crazy ass boyfriend, use to beat her and shit. He was big as hell, no match for me, but we used to fight every time he laid a finger on her. She claimed she was so in love with him, but he wasn't doing shit for her, he wasn't payin' no bills. I took care of that, so he ain't have no place in our house as far as I was concerned. One night me and Zelle was at my house, dude was there but my momma was gone. We got into it and I just shot him, and that was the end of it. My mom moved to California and I moved to Cincinnati with Damen and Zelle two years later." The story about his mom reminded me of my own.

"What did your mom say?"

"She never knew, we moved his body."

"You didn't get caught?"

"Hell na."

"Well, he deserved it," I said, wishing the same thing would happen to Markus.

"Yeah, he did. My momma better off now, she happy in California."

I was silent. I was thinking about my own mom, I wished I could say the same thing about her. But I knew she wasn't happy, she had to be miserable.

"Baby don't worry about it, you gon' get back in touch with yo momma," he said reading my mind.

"Yeah, I know," I said, lying to myself and him.

"I love you." He looked me straight in my eyes again.

"I love you too," I said, trying to crack a smile, but I couldn't. All I could think about was my mom. I wondered what she was doing. Then all of a sudden a guilty feeling came over me. Here I was in Puerto Rico, and she was probably somewhere in some small apartment getting the shit beat out of her. "I'm gonna go back up to the room and lay down," I told Kayne, getting up before he could even respond. Once in the room, I cried until Kayne came in and consoled me. His holding me lead to his kissing me and then his coming inside me, helping me forget all my troubles.

Monday – November 20, 2003

That night we were back in the Nati, and as Kayne put it, back to the grind. We went to Kayne's cousin's place. He didn't think it was safe to go back home yet. He parked the Yukon in the back of the apartment building where it couldn't be seen. I was fine with the idea until I got inside. The apartment was basically a whole in the wall. It was dirty and smelled like old cigarette buds and beer. There were two bedrooms. His cousin's room and an extra room that had nothing in it but and old and dirty futon, and a broken TV that sat on the floor next to the window that overlooked the parking lot. I couldn't believe I went from living in the lap of luxury to staying in a piece of shit.

"How long you plan on staying here?" I asked Kayne as he sat all of our bags down in the corner of the room.

"I don't know, just give me some time to clear my head and think of somethin'." He walked out leaving me standing there, in the middle of the room, I didn't even want to sit down. I studied the room for a minute. I figured if Kayne was planning on staying for a while I could fix it up to suit my needs—sheets for the futon, a new TV, some curtains for the window, and a full size mirror would do it.

Thinking about fixing the room up got my mind on money, something I knew I didn't have a lot of. I knew Kayne had all the money I would need, but with the threat of him being arrested, that money was no guarantee. I thought about what Shayna said about opening an account, but it was too late. I only had $150 left of my own money, and that needed to stay with me. I decided if Kayne gave me a few more stacks, I would stash it.

Kayne appeared in the doorway, interrupting my thought process. "You still standin' there? That futon ain't gon' bite you. Or, you can come in here on the couch with me if you want. I don't bite either." He threw me another one of those sexy grins, and I followed him into the tiny living room that was made up strictly of a couch and TV.

"I'm waitin' on this one nigga to bring me some weed. You smokin?" he asked, already knowing I would. It had become a daily routine for us since I'd lost my baby. "Yeah," I answered. *I need a joint stayin' in this shit whole,* I thought to myself. It was almost like he could read my mind because he looked at me, laughed and shook his head. Then he got up and came back with a white sheet. He told me to stand up and tucked it neatly over the couch.

"Now can you relax a lil' bit?" he said as I finally sat down next to him.

"Thank you."

"Yeah, miss prissy."

"I ain't prissy," I laughed.

"Yeah, ok."

"Where's your cousin?"

"Shit, ain't no tellin with that nigga. He probably won't show up the whole time we here." I didn't comment or ask any questions. I figured that was all I needed to know. "I'm goin' back to the crib tonight to pick up some shit, but I gotta ride out to the garage so we can switch cars. You with me?"

"Un-huh."

"Yeah, you wanna go back and get yo money from Damen, and that lil' jumpsuit you got," he laughed.

"I forgot all about that." I was glad he reminded me about the money, and I knew I would have a letter from Zelle too.

"I ain't forget. I wanna it see on," he told me, referring to the jumpsuit. He pulled me over to him and started kissing me until somebody knocked at the door. It was the person with the weed. He didn't come in, but I could see him from the couch, and I know he saw me quite clearly from the door, because when Kayne handed him the money, he dropped it on the floor trying to sneak a peak at me as I laid on the couch with my breasts damn near popping out of my t-shirt.

I laughed at his clumsiness, but Kayne didn't. He looked at me then back at him. "Come here Mina." He said with his eyes still on the dude at the door, who looked frozen. I got up and walked over to the doorway. "You see her?" Kayne asked almost yelling. He nodded his head nervously. "This me. So whenever you see her, I don't give a fuck where you at, remember this me. Keep yo eyes off her titties, them mine too."

"My bad man, I...ain't mean no dis," he stuttered.

"Man get the fuck outta here," Kayne said slamming the door as dude ran off. I loved the way he handled him, but I didn't say anything. He walked over to the couch and pulled a cigar out of his pocket to roll the weed in.

"I can't stand niggas like that, losing they head over a bitch."

"What!" I couldn't believe what he said.

He looked at me like I was the one who had said something out of line. "I ain't mean it like that, but that's how niggas is. Busy lookin' at ass and titties, instead of takin' care of business. He droppin' money on the floor and shit, I shoulda broke that nigga neck. See if he ever turn his head to look at you again." I watched him roll the joint, then fire it up. He hit it four times before passing it to me. I was heated, but I let the weed get rid of all the tension. Five hits and I was feeling fine. "I ain't mean it like that for real baby, come here," Kayne said pulling me over to him. I nodded to let him know it was ok. He didn't even have to apologize; I would have shook off what he said anyway. He just spoke without thinking first, I know 'cause I did that all the time. After we finished the joint, I let him know he was forgiven by riding him on the couch for a whole hour.

Chapter 18

Monday - November 20, 2003

At 11:30 p.m., we left the shit hole and went to the garage to switch to the Cadillac CTS. Then, we went to Kayne's apartment and for some reason the street was emptier than usual. The middle aged black women that lived next door was sitting on her front steps.

"You ain't seen no police ridin' around here have you?" Kayne asked her on our way to the door.

"Yeah, they been around here a couple of times, them muthafuckas came knockin' on my door askin' did I know where you were and when you would be back. But you know I ain't told them pigs shit. Fuck 'em, you gotta light?"

Kayne reached in his pocket and handed her a lighter. "You can keep it." Quickly he opened the door. Everything in the apartment was just how we left it. Kayne dashed to the bedroom closet and pulled out two huge suitcases, throwing clothes, shoes and jewelry inside. I did the same using my old bags I had under the bed. I made sure to get every last thing. "Come here," he commanded just as I finished packing. I got up from the floor and he led me into his walk-in closet. He lifted up a piece of the carpet in the corner where a pair of his shoes sat; under it was a safe. He entered the combination and opened it revealing neatly packed doe stacks. He started placing the money into a black leather bag. I had never seen so much money in my life. I watched him closely, trying to make an estimate of how much was there, but his swiftness made my eyes lose count. The phone rang, breaking my daze. I got up to go get it.

"Don't answer that." Kayne grabbed me before I could even leave the closet. "Come help me with this money." I did exactly what he said because I knew we were in a hurry. When we were done packing the money, he pulled two black briefcases out of the safe.

"What's that?" I asked.

"Heat," he answered coldly, getting up with the bag and briefcases in hand. "Let's go." He picked up the rest of his bags, and I picked up mine. Then, he led me to the door. I hated to say goodbye to the apartment with all the luxuries it had, but I knew it was either that, or saying goodbye to Kayne a lot sooner than I wanted to.

Before we left, he got the mail out of the mailbox.

"Here." He handed me two envelopes.

Kayne drove the Cadillac and I drove my Lexus. We dragged all of our bags into the extra room as soon as we got back to his cousin's. I heard someone open the other bedroom door as Kayne walked into the living room. I stayed behind trying to situate our bags to give us some walking space.

"Hey Keon. What's up lil' cuz?" I heard a voice yell excitedly.

"What's up?" I heard Kayne reply like he really didn't feel like greeting him.

"I ain't know you was already here, I was thinkin' you was talkin' 'bout next Monday. But look here, I need a lil' somethin' but I ain't got shit right now. I'll pay you back you know that."

"Na, man. I told you I ain't got shit right now. You need to leave that shit alone anyway."

"Aww come on, big time hustler like you, I know you got somethin'."

"I said I ain't got shit."

"Now, don't make me call you out like yo momma use to—Keon Jervonn NaCore!" He laughed loudly imitating a women's voice.

I didn't hear Kayne say anything else; he came back in the room and sat next to me on the futon. His eyes looked the same as they did the day I asked him about his mom, and wished I hadn't. I stared at him, but he didn't look back. He looked straight ahead to the cracked wall in front of us. Leaning over, I gently kissed him on the lips. He kissed me back. Then his cousin appeared in the doorway.

"Who's that in there with you?" He asked, squinting his eyes, straining to see my face in the dark room.

"My girl," Kayne answered in an agitated tone. Unsatisfied with Kayne's answer, his cousin switched on the light and walked over to me.

"Hey pretty. What's yo name?" He put out his hand. He was brown skin with baby dreads; he stood kind of short, and was very thin. He looked about 35, which was a lot older than I expected him to be.

"Amina," I answered, taking his hand trying to be polite. His hands were so dry and scaly; I wanted to pull away from him.

"I'm Jarryl. Nice to meet you, beautiful," he smiled. He was missing so many teeth I couldn't even count how many were absent.

"Nice to meet you too," I politely replied.

He left the room and Kayne got up to get sheets for the futon while I straightened it out. I ended up falling asleep in his arms that night, and his cousin didn't bother us again that night.

Tuesday – November 21, 2003

I woke up looking for Kayne, but he wasn't there. I got up right away to check the apartment for him. Jarryl was sleep on the living room couch.

"Where's Kayne?" I asked shaking him.

"What...Who?" he asked, eyes still closed.

"Kayne. Where is he?"

He sat up and rubbed his eyes then looked at me. "What's wrong pretty? You don't wanna be alone with me? I won't bite you." He pulled my hands trying to get me to sit down. By this time I was irritated.

"Tell me where the fuck Kayne is!" I snapped, pulling away from him. His crooked smile quickly faded.

"They arrested him this mornin'."

"What! When was this?"

"You was sleep, he went outside to get something from the car I guess. Three police cars ran up on him. I was lookin' out my window. I'm sorry baby, he gone." As he was telling me all of this, heavy tears built up in my eyes. But as crazy as this may sound, they never fell.

This is where I come in, I thought. Kayne and I both knew this day was coming, so there was no use in crying. Instead, I decided to make some big moves. I had to prove to him that I was down for him. I was going to do everything in my power to get him out. I went to grab all of my bags from the back. Jarryl helped me carry everything to my car. I was so desperate that I let him drive the Cadillac that was amazingly still there, back to the garage.

I threw him a $50 to go feed his habit and was checked into the West Inn by two o'clock. I figured I had more than enough in the stash to get a room for at least a week. I would do everything I could to avoid getting a job. Like hitting up Damen for a few credit cards, and pawning all of Kayne's expensive jewelry, maybe even selling one of the Cadillacs. I wasn't feeling the idea of filling out applications and kissing some managers ass just to make minimum wage. No 9 to 5 could provide me with money as fast as Damen could, or the streets for that matter. First, I called Shayna to tell her what happened. She was on her way to the hotel right away. Then, I called Damen from the hotel phone.

"Hello?" He answered.

"Daddy?"

"Hey princess, how was the trip? I got the souvenir and post card you mailed. Thanks."

"You're welcome."

"What's wrong? You sound upset."

"It's *Kayne,* he got arrested this morning."

"Where?"

"We were staying at his cousin's on McGregor. They picked him up from there; I left as soon as I found out."

"So, they didn't take possession of the apartment?"

"I don't know. We took all of our clothes out last night. I still have all of Kayne's paper and heat."

"Did you switch cars first?"

"Yeah the CTS. The police didn't even take the car, luckily. His cousin drove it out to the garage for me. I'm in the Lex now."

"How did they find him?"

"I don't know. They had been looking for him for weeks though. Somebody called and warned him before we even got back to Cincinnati. The lady next door said the police came over there asking her questions."

"Where you at now?"

"I got a room at the West Inn."

"Get rid of the guns and keep the money."

"I will," I lied, knowing I would keep at least one.

"I don't like you being alone, why don't you go stay with you're grandma or come to Chicago."

"Daddy, I can't just leave I gotta be here for Kayne."

"Amina, he's in jail."

"So what, so is Zelle. I didn't leave when he got locked up."

"Ok, I just don't feel comfortable with you being alone."

"I'll be fine. Shayna's on her way over here."

"Alright Mina, you're grown. I can't tell you what to do. Oh, Zelle called yesterday, he asked about you. I told him that Kayne had taken you away for your birthday and that I hadn't heard from you yet. He said he sent a letter."

"I got it."

"Alright. How much money you have?"

"I don't know, I ain't counted yet. But I was wondering could I get a couple of credit cards?"

"You mean instead of the checks I send you?"

"Yeah."

"You got the money I sent this month didn't you?"

"Un-huh."

"Yeah. I'll have them sent to the hotel."

"Thanks daddy. I'll call you later."

"I love you, be careful."

"Ok, love you too."

"Girl, I wish I would have known you was gonna need a place to stay a few days earlier. I would have rented you my apartment, but I already rented it to this girl from my job. I gotta go stay with my mom, she ain't doin' good. I would tell her that I changed my mind, but we already signed the papers and everything." Shayna told me as she made her way into the room.

"It's fine. I'll manage."

"You know I really think you should go stay with your grandma."

"Shayna, I can't. I just can't deal with her right now; she'll be all in my business I won't be able to get away."

"I see. Well, what you gon' do…stay in hotels forever? You gon' eventually run out of money."

"I don't know. How long you gon' be in Atlanta?" I changed the subject. I didn't even want to think about the day when I would run out of money.

"Ain't no tellin, probably a few months. She's really not doing too good. I don't know what happened, just last month she was doing fine. She needs somebody there with her and my sister is there 24/7 but she needs a break."

"I hope your mother gets better."

"Yeah, me too. She will though, she's strong."

"When you leavin'?

"Thursday night."

"Does Damen know?"

"Yeah, I just told him this morning."

"I just got off the phone with him."

"I bet he had a fit, he's probably worried to death about you." Shayna took a seat on the huge king size bed.

"Un-huh. He tried to get me to go to my grandma's too, or come stay with him. But I need to be here so I can know what's going on with Kayne."

"I understand." She grabbed her purse and pulled out her checkbook. "Here, this is just something to add to your stash, and don't forget about opening that account."

"I won't. I was gonna go tomorrow. But you really don't have to give me anything. I'm fine."

"Girl, you gon' take this check, here." She ripped it from the checkbook and handed it to me.

"Thank you," I said reluctantly.

Shayna had written it out for four hundred dollars. She got up to give me a hug.

"I would stay longer, but I gotta go pack. I ain't even started yet. I'll call you before I leave. Be careful, and please stay in school...please." She looked me in my eyes and ran her hand down my hair.

"Ok, thanks Shayna, for everything."

"You're welcome, Amina," she smiled. "Call me if you need anything else. My plane doesn't leave until 11 p.m."

"Alright." I got up to let her out.

Once she was gone, I counted the money in the leather bag. There was only fifteen thousand I was shocked, this was chump change to Kayne. Was this his only stash? When I added my $150, the four hundred from Shayna, and five hundred from Damen my total was $16,050. That wasn't that much after considering my hotel room was $110 a night and I planned on staying at least a week.

I told myself to just relax and worry about things tomorrow. I ordered some room service and I took a hot bath. In the tub, I read the letter from Zelle.

Dear Amina,

I know I told you I would write you on your birthday, but I promise this won't be the only letter you get from me. How are things holding up? Good, I hope. I hope your birthday was as special as I would have made it if I was home. But I'm guessing Kayne did a decent enough job making you happy.

I wish I could be home just to see your bright smile. I miss you more than any nigga in here miss anybody. I'm all fucked up not knowing what's going on with my lil' sister. I need to be able to call you anytime day or night, to know you still breathing.

All the pain you been through in the past months makes me even more noided. You don't deserve shit, but the best. Remember that, and don't fuck with nobody that can't give you that.

Everyday I think about how short our time was together, it's real fucked up and I'm sorry for that. I should've been smarter, did things different, but because I didn't this is where I'm at. I hope you not mad at me, even though you got more than enough reason to be.

Maybe shit will work out. I go to court on the 24th. I want you to be in the courtroom, so I can see your face. That will be enough to put me at ease even if I am thrown ten years.

Stay up and be smart. You know what I mean. I love you.

> *Your brother,*

> *Azelle*

As soon as I finished crying and got out of the tub, I got a call on my cell phone. "Hello?"

"Amina?" It was Terrance.

"It's me."

"I just talked to Damen about Zelle, his court date is the 24th. I pulled some strings and managed to have him see a judge I'm real close with. He'll be out by May. I just wanted to call and let you know."

"For real?" I couldn't believe how fast things were moving.

"Yeah, but you have to keep this between me, you and Damen. If you write Zelle don't mention it. It would help, too, if you just showed up to court normal."

"Oh, of course. I understand. Thank you so much." I was grateful for his help. Now all I needed was to get up the nerve to ask him to help out with Kayne.

"Ok, I'm gonna take your word on that."

"How much do I owe you."

"Damen's already taken care of it."

"Alright. Um, before you go, I was wondering if you could help me out with one more situation." I hoped I wasn't pressing my luck.

"What's that?"

"I need to get my boyfriend out. He got arrested today on almost the same charges as Zelle."

"A crack case?"

"Yeah."

"What's his name?"

"Well, his real name is Keon. You know him. He used to work for you, I don't know if you remember."

"Keon? Lil' dirty Keon?"

"He's far from dirty now," I said respectfully correcting him, defending Kayne but trying not to turn Terrance off from helping me.

"So, Keon's got a little name for himself now. Kayne," he laughed "I taught that boy well," he said proudly.

"Yeah, he told me." I said sucking up, hoping it would help. "So, do think you might be able to pull some strings for him too? I'm willing to do just about anything," I said desperately.

"You must be in love," he laughed.

"I am."

"Damen knows about this?" he asked, laughing again. I was starting to get irritated. It seemed like he was trying to avoid the question, but I stayed humble.

"He knows," I told him, giving off a little chuckle in return.

"Be careful, these young boys are a trip. I don't wanna see my lil' cousin get hurt."

"I will, but I'll break down if they put him away for some years."

"I don't know if I can pull off another one of these stunts for a while. I can't do them too close together. Maybe after Zelle's out, I can try something with Keon."

When Zelle's out? That's almost seven whole months away, I thought, biting my tongue. "Alright," I managed to reply.

"And maybe you should think about leaving these drug dealers alone. They get you caught up. What about a nice guy with a job, or a college boy maybe?"

I was past ready to get off the phone; his playing the father role wasn't helping at all. "I'll think about that," I lied. I wasn't thinking about anybody, but Kayne. I was determined to get him out whether I had Terrance's help or anyone else's.

"Ok, baby girl. Call me and let me know that everything went smoothly."

"I will. Thanks again."

"No problem."

Chapter 19

Wednesday – November 22, 2003

First thing in the morning, I called Damen to tell him that I would be leaving the West Inn and to send the credit cards to the Holiday Inn Express on Mitchell Avenue. The West Inn was too expensive. I ran a few errands before switching hotels. First, I went to pay my phone bill, which was $152, and then I went to Hide Park to open an account at Provident Bank. I deposited six thousand into a savings account. I was careful not to put too much in at once. I didn't want to draw attention to myself. That left me with $9,885. As I pulled the money stacks from my Coach bag, I noticed the clerk give me a funny look.

"A lot of money there," she commented, with her eyes glued to the money.

"Yeah," I laughed. "I asked my dad to just write me a check." She laughed in return. She seemed to lighten up after I fed her a little bullshit. But I was glad.

As I was pulling the last of the money out, a folded piece of paper fell out. It was the list of names Kayne had written out for me. I had completely forgotten about it, and I didn't even remember putting it in there. Good thing Kayne planned ahead. Next stop, the pawn shop to get rid of his guns.

As soon as I walked in, the clerk jumped to my service. "What can I help you with today, beautiful?" He acted like he had never had a customer before. "What you got there? Let's take a look." I opened the cases; he carefully looked over each gun. "I'll give you five hundred for them."

"Five hundred? There's five guns here. The chopper alone is worth that much and I'm not selling the .22," I informed him.

"Well then, it'll be four hundred."

"You can come up with a little bit more than that. I'm giving you two nine's, a chopper, and two AK's."

"That's one hundred each." I began to close the cases. He grabbed my hand. "Do you really think you're gonna find a better deal?" He asked.

"Seven hundred." I argued.

"Six." He said pulling the guns towards him.

"Six-fifty."

"Ok," he agreed, he went to the cash register and counted out the money in my hand. He handed me the .22; I placed it in my bag.

"I wouldn't keep that there," he warned.

"Yeah," I said rolling my eyes, walking out. I knew I had let him milk me, and I didn't even know why. I guess I was just desperate; selling the guns on the street would have been hot. I was taking no risk. After checking into the Holiday Inn Express, I was heading up to my room when I got a call.

"Hello?" I answered.

"Yes, is this Amina Costello?"

"Yeah, who is this?"

"My name is Thomas Fillmont. I'm Keon's attorney. I'm calling to let you know what's going on."

"Ok, I'm listening."

"Keon is under investigation right now; you know…the car, apartment, all of that. If they find anything it can add time, but right now we're looking at four years. There's really no evidence at all right now. But for someone without a nine to five, that's evidence enough. He doesn't have visible means of income, which is never good."

"Un-huh," I agreed, listening for something I didn't already know.

"Now police say they've been watching him for a long time, so they know for sure that he's been involved in drug activity, there's no getting around that. But as far as them actually finding drugs, we're doing pretty well. We just need to work on the four years."

"Ok, so say they do throw him three years, there's no kind of bail?"

"Depends on how well I represent him. If I can convince the court to give him a second chance, the bail could be anywhere from three to five thousand."

"What? For a little drug case?"

"Actually, this is a big drug case. Keon is just one of 23 people who were arrested in the last two weeks. Now, usually everybody would just be thrown in jail and that would be the end of it. However, since there are so many people, bails are being extremely high. Basically, they're just trying to make some money off of these drug dealers because they know they have it. It's crazy, I know, but that's the reality of it."

"So what's your fee?"

"Seven thousand. That covers unlimited court appearances.

In Keon's case we may go to court about three or four times, and considering how many people have cases it may be a while before he even gets a court date. The longer it takes, the higher I charge. After two weeks it goes up five hundred every week."

"Don't you think that's kind of steep? What if we lose, you keep all of the money and I'm left with nothing for bail either?"

"Well, if we lose there won't be bail and if that should happen you would be reimbursed half of the money. But let's not think of us losing this case."

"No. Let's do, and what the hell is all this we shit? The only we is Keon and me. If you ain't paid, you not even in, so cut the bullshit."

"Ms. Costello, I will do everything in my power to avoid Keon getting a long sentence. But, you have to understand that when people get themselves into situations like this, they can't get themselves out and have to pay someone to help. That someone for you and Keon is me. I've been a lawyer for eight years, and have only lost two cases in those eight years. I'm pretty sure unless you call Johnny Cochran; you're not going to get much better than that."

I sat on the phone, quite for a long time. "Where's Keon? I need to talk to him, can't he make phone calls."

"Not to a cell phone. But I'm going to the jail tomorrow morning. I'll have him call on my phone."

"Ok, make sure you do that." I hung up before the conversation could go any further. Immediately, I called Damen and told him everything. Of course he advised me to just leave Kayne alone.

"He dug himself in this whole alone. You shouldn't be breaking your neck to get him out." What he didn't understand was that I was in love, and willing to do break every bone in my body to keep Kayne from doing three years in jail, I knew he could do the time, I just knew I couldn't. I didn't tell Damen that though.

I knew I had to work alone, because nobody cared whether Kayne ever saw sunlight again. Not even his money hungry lawyer.

Thursday – November 23, 2003

I was up early this morning writing Zelle back when Kayne called. "Hello?"

"What up baby, you aight?"

"Kayne?" I asked, as if I didn't believe it was him.

"Yeah, it's me. How you holdin' up?"

"Fine, I guess. What about you?"

"I'm just waitin'. That's all a nigga can do is sit and wait for something to happen." The conversation was so casual. He was talking like he was already serving four years time. I was expecting him to give me some important instructions.

"So you want me to pay the lawyer this seven thousand plus the five hundred?" I led the conversation to where I wanted it to go.

"I'ma see if I can get him to come down a lil' bit."

"Why don't you just get another lawyer, he charge too damn much Kayne."

"I know baby, but he one of the best in the city and it's gon' be hard to find another one right now. I'm lucky to have him; most of these niggas in here don't even have one."

"I can try to find one."

"Where you stayin' at?"

"The Holiday Inn on Mitchell. I was at the West Inn for a night, but that was breakin' me."

"Why don't you go stay with Shayna for a while?"

"She rented her place out. Plus, she's going to Atlanta for a few months. Her momma's sick."

"Oh. How much money you got?"

"Six stacks in the bank, $10,570 with me."

"I don't think this shit gon' work. Money is low and you need to get a place and have money to eat and shit. I might just let them give me these years. I knew this shit was comin' anyway."

"What? What you mean let it go? I'll get the money. Damen's sending me credit cards that'll help. And what about that list? Who you want me to call? If they can get me some work, I'll have the money in no time."

"Every nigga on that list is in here. It's over Mina, just take the money and get you a place. I don't want you livin' in hotels."

"No. I'll get the money." Tears began building up in my eyes. I couldn't believe he was giving up just like that.

"What you know about hustlin' anyway? You crazy if you think I'ma have you out there like that. It ain't worth you riskin' yo life. I'll be aight. I been in jail before, and three years ain't shit. That's vacation time."

"Well it won't be no fuckin' vacation for me! I was willin' to do anything just to keep you outta jail, and now you just wanna say fuck it?" It was clear that I was crying now, you could hear it in my voice.

"Go get you a place like I said. I gotta go, I love you, and stop cryin'. This ain't the last you gon' hear from me. I love you, Mina," he hung up.

I slept until Shayna called and woke me up. She wanted to meet me for dinner that night at J. Alexander's around six; her treat. I agreed. After dinner, we said our goodbyes, she gave me her mother's number, and then I went to mail Zelle's letter. My next mission was to head out to the garage to check on the cars. I was planning on selling both the Cadillac's.

When I discovered a completely empty garage, I thought for sure I would die. I dropped to the floor in disbelief. Not only were the Cadillac's gone, but the Yukon too. I was sitting in the middle of a dirty garage floor in my $500 cream Dolce and Gabbana pants and didn't give a damn. I couldn't move or think. I could only sit there. I didn't even want to know who took the cars, because I would have been in jail right along with Kayne. Only my case would be murder.

"Damn, what happened here?" I heard a voice say. I turned around, it was Derrick.

"I don't know." I answered still in shock.

"You just gon' sit on the ground like that, and get all dirty?" He reached his hand out, and pulled me up from the floor. I looked at the back of my pants they were filthy.

"What you doin' here?"

"I got storage out here I came to look for somethin'. I seen yo car."

"Oh," I sighed looking over at his black Acura.

"So where ya mans at?" I just looked at him. I was too embarrassed to answer. After playing him like I did, he would probably get a good laugh. "Oh, none of my business huh?"

"He's in jail," I finally answered looking away. I couldn't stand to see a satisfied look on his face.

"Damn, I'm sorry. I know you was real serious 'bout that nigga. I seen it when I tried to get at you. That's fucked up; alot of my niggas got locked up too. It's a big ass drug bust goin' on. It's bout to be a drought out here. I smell it." I was grateful he didn't act stupid about the situation.

173

"Yeah. I was gonna sell the cars to get extra money. I gotta get somewhere to stay and pay the lawyer."

"Damn. They out to get niggas for real this time. This shit just a big ass fundraiser."

"Hell yeah. It's crazy. I don't know what the fuck to do now."

"The Feds probably came and took them cars. You know they can do that. They take everything you got."

"I know."

"How much money you tryna make?"

"Fifteen."

"Oh that's nothin' shorty. I can get you that in three weeks, but you gotta work for it."

"Aight. I'm down, just tell me what I gotta do." I had some idea what he meant.

"Follow me home."

I followed him to Alexandria apartments on Gilbert Avenue. I called Fillmont right away and told him he would get his money, and that I expected Kayne to get off the hook. He agreed. First, Derrick taught me how to make rocks. We worked on them for two hours. It took me a while to get the hang of it. When two licks called him, he gave them to me.

One was a lady about 45. She wore some green and black polk-a-dot stretch pants, with light up L.A. gears, and a pink shirt that made her stand out like a bottle of Pepto Bismol. I sold her two ounces in Derrick's hallway.

The other was a tall light-skinned man with a speech impediment. I could barely understand what he was saying, but Derrick helped me out by translating his words. By 12:30 p.m., I was on my way back to the hotel with seven hundred extra dollars in my pocket. Derrick kept me up on licks. By Sunday night

I had made two more stacks. I planned on giving Fillmont a down payment after Zelle's sentencing, that Monday. I began searching the newspapers for an apartment. I circled an advertisement for a one-bedroom apartment in Forest Park, $650 a month.

Triple Crown Publications presents

Chapter 20

Monday - November 24, 2003

I had to let Zelle know that I was still holding it down, even with him being locked up. I was hoping to make him proud. I wore a tan Bebe dress suit, with a silk pink camisole and pointed toe sling backs that went perfect with the suit. My hair was down in soft curls, and my nails were done in French manicure. I looked classier than I ever had before; it was a different look for me.

It was early, eight a.m., but the courtroom was packed. There were six cases before Zelle's. Finally, I saw him. They brought him in along with two other prisoners. All of them had their hands and feet cuffed. It hurt so bad to see Zelle like that. The police officers handled him like he was an animal, jerking and pulling on his chains.

He didn't see me right away because I was in the third row sort of hidden in the thick crowd. But I'll never forget the look he gave me when our eyes did finally meet.

I smiled at him with confidence. He smiled back, but with nervousness. He had no idea he had already been let off the hook. I know he had to be noided. His hair had grown out, his waves were gone, it was curly now. He still looked cute.

He stared at me for a long time. I stared back wondering what he was thinking about. I wanted to hug him and talk to him so bad. The fact that I couldn't, tortured the hell out of me.

When the judge called his name, he stood up with his court appointed lawyer—a short white lady with red curly hair, in a cheap suit, and even cheaper shoes. She looked every bit of a lawyer as Markus did.

I got butterflies in my stomach when it came time for the judge to read Zelle's sentence.

"Azelle Costello, I'm sentencing you to seven months in the justice center."

When Zelle turned around, he looked completely relieved. I was too. His lawyer looked confused like something had gone wrong. The officer led Zelle out of the courtroom. He turned to me and smiled; this time with confidence. I mouthed to him "I love you." He returned the gesture and then he was gone.

After I left the courtroom, I sat in Busken's Bakery feeling good. I ordered a breakfast sandwich. Then I called Terrance, like he had told me too. When I hung up with him I called Damen.

"So, the judge came through huh?"

"Yeah. Thank God." I smiled in between bites of my sandwich.

"Terrance said she would."

"I know, I'm so happy." I could understand why Terrance said he and the judge were close. She was a very attractive brown skin woman. The connection was obvious.

"Me too, so what's up, what you doin now?"

"Well, I'm gonna go back to the hotel and lay down for a while after I leave Busken's. Then I gotta be back downtown by 3:30 to meet Kayne's lawyer."

"You haven't looked at any apartments."

"I'm thinking about one in Forest Park."

"You get the two credit cards I sent?"

"Yeah. I got them Friday. Thanks."

"Ok. Call me when you get a place. And try to get one soon."

"I will."

"I love you."

"I love you too." We hung up.

On my way to the car, Derrick called. "I got some work for you," he said.

"Aight. What's up?"

"I need you to make a big drop for me downtown on Main Street. I would do it, but dude won't be here to pick it up 'til two and I gotta go to Louisville to re-up."

"I'm down here now. You said at two?"

"Yeah, this shit is worth five. You can keep three."

"Aight, so does he know I'm gonna be droppin it off?"

"Yeah. His name is Red. It'll be a lil' white dude with him. Red drives a black Town Car.

"So, I give it to Red?"

"Yeah. I'ma leave my door unlocked. It'll be a black leather bag under the sink in the cabinet. Come in here, get it and lock the door back. When you get the money come back and slide the two stacks in my mail chute."

"I got it. So where on Main?"

"Right in front of that lil' corner store by 13th street, going towards Liberty."

"Aight."

I had some time to waste so I went back to the hotel and waited until 1:30 before leaving. I was feeling good, so I decided to stay looking good in my suit and pumps. I went to Derrick's and followed the exact directions he gave me. I drove down to Main and parked in front of the corner store. The neighborhood was unusually quiet. But the sun was out, and it was warm with a calming breeze. I thought about Kelly and Trina. I knew they were in school. *Maybe I should go back,* I thought as I waited for Red.

It was exactly two o'clock when I saw the black Lincoln Town Car pull up behind me through the rearview. I didn't get out, I waited. Who I assumed was Red walked slowly to my car. He was dressed in all black—sweater, slacks, and gators. A nice Rolex was on his wrist. He looked about 28 or 29. I was expecting younger, but it didn't bother me. He had five thousand dollars for me and I was ready for my three thousand cut.

"You're Amina?" He asked with a serious tone.

"Yeah, and you're Red?"

"Yeah." I handed him the bag through the window.

"What's a girl like you doing in this kind of business?"

"Long story." I looked through the rearview again and saw a white guy step out of the Town Car, holding a conversation on his cell phone.

"Be careful," Red said placing a stack of money in my hand. I counted it out, the right amount was there.

"I always am," I said flirtatiously, giving him a sly smile. He flashed one back, and I started my car and began to drive back up the street heading to Derrick's. As I passed the first block leading out to Liberty Street, two police cars turned from around the corner, surrounding me and causing me to swerve to the left side of the street.

"Stop the vehicle!" They shouted. Two more police cars raced up to the scene. All eight officers had guns pointed directly at me. I was stuck with no way out. I slowly got out of the car with my hands in the air.

A female officer that I didn't notice at first cuffed me and read me my rights. I was facing fifteen years in jail, just for the ten kilos of crack that was in the black bag. After they found the twenty-two that was in my trunk, I was surely facing 21 years, no bail. Luckily it wasn't loaded, that would have added years.

"Yeah. Derrick knew exactly what he was doing. He got out of here fast, and left you to get busted," the lady officer as she led me into the female section of the justice center.

"What?" I said.

"Sweetie, I know you don't think that was all a mistake. Derrick knew exactly what was going to happen today that's why he sent you. Lucky him, he's probably somewhere across the border by now. It's so sad, I see so many girls like you. They get set up, and end up spending the rest of their lives in here." I was speechless. There were no words. Nothing I could say would change how things turned out...nothing.

After they placed me in a cell with a 27-year-old dyke with cornrows, I broke down. I didn't get to call Damen for three whole nights, and every one of those nights I had to fight off my cell mate, Deena, or as I called her, David, but never to her face.

A guard finally had mercy on me and moved me to a cell with a Puerto Rican girl whose story was a lot like mine.

The fourth morning I finally called Damen. "What the fuck was you doing selling crack!" He yelled when I explained the whole story.

"I needed fast money." I told him.

"Fast money! Look where fast money got you, the same place your brother is."

"I know, I need yo help."

"I'll call Terrance."

"Ok." I mumbled.

"Call me back whenever you can. I love you. Just hang in there for a while."

"Alright. I love you too."

Damen flew in that week to visit. He told me that he and Terrance were working on it. A month later, in mid-December, I got a visit from Shayna. She was back from Atlanta and her mom was doing better. She still looked good, and I hated her for it. She told me that Damen was taking her to Italy for her birthday in a few weeks and how she always wanted to go there. In February, she was moving to Chicago to be with him. I pretended to be happy for her, but I really just wanted to scream and let out all the anger, and pain.

Chapter 21

Thursday - December 10, 2003

It's was exactly two weeks before Christmas, and the line for the phone seemed a mile long. There were twelve people in front of me, and three times as many behind me. When my turn was up, I dialed my grandmother's number. When she didn't answer, I began to dial Damen's number. The sign over the phone clearly read, *"One Call per Person,"* but I didn't care, I needed to get in touch with someone about getting me a lawyer. "Daddy pick up." I said after the tone from the operator informing him of my collect call. He accepted.

"Hey baby." He greeted me, just as I felt a harsh shove in my back.

"Bitch, you illiterate? The sign say one phone call!" I turned around to an angry dark skinned bitch with one gold and corn rows braided tightly to the back.

I wasn't intimidated. I rolled my eyes and continued to talk on the phone. "Daddy, did you talk to my grandma about a lawyer yet?" I asked desperately.

"A yo Cola! This bitch must be deaf too!" Another chick standing behind me shouted to the girl who had just pushed me.

"Amina, is everything alright? If you need to call me later, I'll be here." Damen asked sounding concerned.

"No! Fuck that, this is important, they can wait just like I did!" I shouted loud enough for the whole line to hear. Cola grabbed the hand I was holding the phone with, and I struggled with her. She eventually won the arm wrestle and hung it up.

"I been waitin' long enough, it's my turn!" She picked up the phone again to dial out. I wrapped both of my arms around her neck in a serious attempt to choke her to death. I wasn't smart about my approach. I should have waited until I caught her alone, because all of a sudden, I felt a huge amount of weight on my back. Two of her girls had nearly jumped on my back trying to pull me off of her. I finally gave up on choking Cola and turned around to fight the other two girls who looked almost identical to her—big ugly bitches. I hit both of them in the face, swinging my fights around with all the force I had. When blood splattered from one girl's mouth, I knew I was all the way through. Cola swung me into the cement wall so hard, I felt like a semi had hit me from behind. The other two followed up with face and body shots. The pain from the blows quickly drained me of the energy to block my face or fight back.

A heavyset brown-skinned older woman approached and began pulling the three girls off of me, one by one. My mind felt relief, but my body felt broken in half. I wondered how one chick managed to pull three girls away from me without them fighting back. And where the fuck were the prison guards? Didn't they hear people chanting "Fight! Fight!?" Didn't they hear my body slam into the wall? Or the sound of four fists hitting my face, while two more pounded at my stomach? If they wouldn't protect me in this earthly hell, who would?

Thursday - December 15, 2003

I think it's been five days since I've been in solitary. Just weeks ago I was sitting on a beach with Kayne thanking God for blessed me, little ol' unlucky Amina with someone who truly loved and cared for me. In fact, it's those days with Kayne that have proven to be my saving grace in here. I close my eyes and hear the waves; I see his face and feel his touch. As I sit on the inside of these tiny four walls, the whole world is continuing without me. I wonder what Kelly and Trina are doing. How their senior year of high school is going. I wonder if it started snowing or what my hair looks like. I haven't seen myself in days and I know my face is fucked up from the fight. I probably should have gotten some medical treatment. I probably need stitches. I hope it don't get one of those nasty scars. I want to look good when I get out of here and see Kayne.

Monday – December 21, 2003

I wonder if my family forgot about me. Do they know that I'm even in the hole? My mother…hell, I don't even know where she is. If I'm going through like this after being in here for a couple of days, how the hell am I going to handle 21 years? When I get out of here I should just drop dime on everyone and work out a deal. I could snitch on my dad. I haven't know him but for like what, six months. Six months compared to the seventeen years he wasn't in my life ain't shit. He need to be sitting in here instead of me just for that. What about Zelle, he killed mad people. I can tell the cops that Damien and Zelle kidnapped me and forced me to deal drugs for them. I can even get Brag to testify how Zelle came to my mother's house and beat her man up. I can say that's when he kidnapped me.

What the hell am I talking about? *Amina, girl, you are losing your mind. You can't rat on them. Sad as it may be, they are the only family you have right now and you need them to get you out of this.* I know…you're right. I need them and I'll never snitch on them after all they've done for me. No one forced me to sell them drugs. I have no one to blame but me.

Thursday - Christmas Eve

Freedom! Well sort of. I got out this morning and I couldn't wait to brush my teeth, wash my face and find a mirror. During lunch, I spotted the woman who helped me when I was jumped. I waited until I saw her sit down and I joined her after getting my tray. "Hey," I stood across from her holding my tray. "I just wanted to say thanks for looking out. Them bitches had my ass." I felt awkward thanking a complete stranger, but I owed it to her.

"Yeah, I just hate to see somebody bein' jumped, that shit ain't cool," she said nonchalantly, taking a bite out of her sandwich. "I was taught to fight fair. Cola could have went one on one with you. You know? You probably would of beat her ass," she laughed, cracking me a smile that reminded me of Kelly. She motioned for me to take a seat. Immediately I became more at ease and sat down.

"I wanna meet that bitch alone somewhere. See how big she is then," I said meaning every word. Two week in hell and you would have thought I'd learn my lesson.

"You just gotta have somebody you stick with in here. Whether it's one person or four, you gotta have somebody. It don't matter how long you here either, it can be eight days or eight years, you just gotta have some kind of back up. I'm pretty cool with Cola and her little clique, but they take advantage of girls they're jealous of. That's how it is in jail or out. Anyway, I'm Sondra, but you can call me Sonny. "

"Ok, I'm Amina."

"What you in for?" she asked.

"Drug trafficking," I answered trying not to make it sound so harsh.

"Sounds familiar." She looked disgusted by the thought.

"Yeah, I'm lookin' at 21 years. I don't know why they would give me that long for my first offense."

"Shit, they'll do just about anything. Never underestimate. I did three years for the same shit in January of '97 and I'm right back in."

"You in for the same thing right now?"

"Wish it was the same. Right now I gotta murder rap, with four bodies on my name." A shiver went through me, and my jaws nearly dropped to the floor. I tried my hardest not to seem alarmed. She looked so innocent, like the girl next door. Despite her size, she was very pretty. Her skin was almost flawless, and the way she wore her hair pulled back in one afro-puff gave her a certain glow. She reminded me a lot of Jill Scott. Her appearance made her seem wise, like a sort of older sister you could run to.

"Four bodies? How did you get into that?" I finally managed to ask.

"It wasn't me, I'm far from a killer. It's a long story," she smiled with sadness in her eyes. I felt relief and suddenly wanted to know more.

"I'm listening, I got all the time in the world right now."

"Ok...where do I begin?" She closed her eyes as if recalling an exact event. "I guess I should start with the day I met my first love, Dorian." She smiled at the thought of his name. I thought of Kayne and my heart sank. I blocked his name out of my mind and concentrated on Sonny's words. They had met when they were kids at her best friends party. She was only eleven and he was thirteen. Dorian was a stick up kid and a Crip and by the time the two of them had been together for six years, he had become a hitman for local dope boys, hence his nickname "Hits." Sonny didn't really have a family. After she finished high school, she moved into an apartment with her boyfriend.

"After two years of living with Dorian, the fairy tale was over. He became extremely abusive. He wanted me home all the time, because he was insecure. If I would leave to go to the store, I had to ask him first. It was crazy, but I tried to convince myself that I was happy because the money was good. But you can't fake happiness, at least not for too long."

"Where you from?" I was starting to hear her accent.

"Compton."

"So, I'm confused. How did you end up here?"

"Well, I caught both of my cases behind Dorian. I was broke. We had broken up and he told me the only way to get back together was if I sold for him. I got caught and did three years. That was in Cali. Then when I got out I left him and moved here with one of my homegirls from high school. He found me and decided that he wanted to set up shop in Cincinnati. Things were cool between us for about a year and then he got into some shit with some local cats. I mean some real gangsta shit. They wasn't trying to hear no parts of some Cali Crip nigga coming in and taking over. A war started. Dorian did a drive by in my fuckin' car and I got pinned with the murders. " As she told her story, I tried to imagine myself in her shoes. Maybe my life wasn't as bad as I thought. "The feds tried to cut me a deal, saying that if I gave names I would only get three to five. But Dorian had instilled loyalty in me since day one, so my mouth was sealed shut."

"Where was the shooting?" By now I was sitting on the edge of my seat and hadn't touch my food.

"In Avondale on July 8th. You had to have heard about it on the news."

"Yeah, I think I did."

"And the most fucked up thing was how I found out." Sonny said taking a sip of her drink.

"Why, what happened?"

"I was on my way to work and I was rushing. I ran a red light and got pulled over, at seven thirty in the damn morning. I reached in the glove compartment for my license and registration. I hated police so I always kept that shit handy. As I felt around for the papers I had my eyes glued to my rearview watching the cop run my plates. My fingers immediately touched the gun and that's all it took. The cop found some other dirt Dorian had done on my plates and decided to search my car. And I don't have to tell you the rest."

"Didn't it have his prints too?"

"Dorian wasn't that dumb. He always used gloves, the gun was clean until I laid hands on it."

"What happened to Dorian?"

"Them niggas caught up with them. Dorian was shot three times in the head while he was sitting in a McDonald's drive thru. So, enough about me. Tell me your story," she said, scooting closer with interest. It took me by surprise, I'd never had a chance to tell anybody my story. I took the opportunity starting from the day I got the letter from Damen, to the day I was arrested. I left out the part about hiring Shadow to kill Amber. I felt close to Sonny, but I had just learned from her story to trust no one.

That night, I got on my knees and prayed for the first time in months. I had been holding a grudge against God ever since I left my mom's house, and I was finally ready to let go of it. It was hard to pray over the sound of my cellmate snoring and the two dykes in the next cell making noises as they played with each other, but I managed.

As bad as I wanted to beg God for mercy, I decided not to. I felt like I didn't deserve it. I hadn't spoken to him in so long; I didn't want to be one of those people who only prayed when they were in trouble. Instead, I apologized for all the wrong I had done. I apologized for getting Amber killed, and not stopping Zelle and Kayne from killing Steelo. I apologized for selling drugs, I even apologized for leaving home. I could have saved my mother from whatever she was going through now. Instead, I left her over a petty argument. I knew how my mother was when it came to men, she fell in love fast because she was lonely. I could have looked past the hurtful things she said and been strong for her because I knew she was becoming weak again. I was starting to realize that I was selfish. Everything always had to be convenient for me, I never gave God a chance to settle my problems. Instead of praying that Amber wouldn't snitch, I got her killed. Instead of praying that Zelle would get out, I went and took things in my own hands. I was always taught to pray in times of need, and that God always answers prayers. Where had my morals gone? Why didn't I just put my trust in him? As I prayed with tears streaming down my face, I began to hate myself. I had become my own worst enemy, and I had never felt this way in my life.

Chapter 22

Friday - Christmas Day

"Moore! You have a visitor!" yelled the male guard. My grandmother came to visit, just as she promised. As soon as I sat down with her, shame came over me, and I avoided her eyes.

"Hi Grandma, Merry Christmas." I wanted to hug and kiss her.

"Merry Christmas, Amina. I brought you some things." She patted the thick package on her lap.

I smiled again. "Thank you. Have you talked to my mom?"

"She left me a message on Thanksgiving. When I called her number back it was disconnected, I haven't heard from her since. But don't worry about it baby, I'm gonna find your mama, and she's gonna bring her ass home and be here for you," she said sternly, as she found the pain in my eyes.

"Does she know I'm here?"

"No, she probably thinks your still living the good life with Damen. She feels like you chose him over her, and she's the one who raised you. But I told her she can't blame you for wanting to get close to your father; I just think she was hurt by it." My guilt became heavier. "But I found a lawyer by the name of John Witman, he's really expensive, but really good."

"My dad will pay for everything, grandma."

"Well, it might be better if I just took care of the lawyer. See, he wants to cut you a deal Mina."

"What kind of deal?" I knew my own grandma wasn't selling me out.

"The police want information about Kayne, and the person that they call his *connect*." She was talking to me like I didn't know street terms. "They may want information about your brother too, but they most likely won't bring him up. They basically need more dirt on Kayne and his connect, do you know who he is?"

"I ain't givin' no information to nobody about Kayne *or* Zelle. I got here trying to help Kayne, why would I turn on him now?" I was beyond pissed at the thought of becoming a snitch.

"To help yourself Amina! You're 18 years old facing 21 years! Before you moved out of your mama's house, you wouldn't have dreamed of getting' in a mess like this. Whose fault do you think that is? Damen should have been watching out for you, but instead he left you here. If he cared he would have *made* you go to Chicago, or come stay with me, not send you to live with some no good nigga that never worked a job a day in his life! If you love him fine! But you better love yourself first baby girl, cause nobody will do it better!" With that, she furiously jumped up from her seat and handed the guard my package. I sat there dumbfounded with her words still lingering in my head.

My cellmate was still on a visit, so I headed back to my cell and ripped opened my package right away. Inside was a set of brand new white sheets, two white bath towels, a pair of white house slippers, and a white terry cloth robe. I put the sheets on my tattered mattress and secured the towels underneath it. I slipped into my robe and slippers and laid down to think about my options. They were simple, snitch on Kayne and his connect Wess, or stay true and do my time. If I threw dirt on Kayne's name he would only suffer more. Sure, I was facing way more time than him, but Kayne never put a gun to my head and told me to do what I did. I had made my own bed, now I had to lay in it. I was starting to realize what Kayne was facing wasn't that bad at all. I could have waited three years if I had to, and worked to make us a home. But I didn't; now I'm stuck. My only hope was Damen and Savellman, because I sure wasn't taking no punk ass deal with the Feds.

January 1, 2004

I told Sonny about what my grandma wanted me to do. "Kayne never did anything to hurt you, so don't hurt him now. He cared enough to warn you about what you were getting your-self into when it was just an idea in your head. He loved and supported you when you didn't have your mom. He even kept you in school when you felt like giving up. Be grateful for that. You have to make your own decision, but don't be mad at your grandmother cause she loves you. I don't think she has anything against Kayne, she's just trying to save you, and you can't expect her to save the both of you. She's on your side." We ate our lunch together like we did everyday but today everything Sonny said made sense and I was confident I was making the right choice.

I was surprised when I got a visit from Kelly that day. After we both sat down, we stared at each other, for what seemed like forever. She had changed so much. Her hair was cut short and dyed bright red. She always could wear the hell out of some red. She broke the awkward silence first. "Amina, I'm sorry for what-ever kept us from speaking, but I can't leave you alone now. It wouldn't be right."

I couldn't believe I was crying when I felt tears run down my face. I tried to wipe them away, until I realized that Kelly had started crying to, then it didn't matter. "I'm sorry too, it was all so petty. But it's over now." She smiled and wiped her eyes. I did the same. "You doin' that haircut girl." I laughed trying to light-en the mood.

"Thanks. Shawn's been wanting me to cut it for the longest, I don't know why. Trina's cousin did it, you remember Tasha."

"Yeah, where is Trina? And what's up with you and Shawn now?"

"She's out of town, she told me to get your information so she can write you. She misses you just as much as I do. We don't go out as much anymore, since you been gone. And me and Shawn just moved in together about a month ago."

"Where yaw stayin'?"

"Evanston right now but we looking for somewhere else. It's getting kind of hot out there."

"Kelly, be careful. Please don't get caught up," I warned her.

"I won't," she smiled with sympathy, and I felt so low. I was the bad ending, the example to be smarter. "So, what's going on you gotta lawyer?"

"I just found out they want to cut me a deal, they want information about Kayne. I don't know what to do," I said helplessly.

"Amina, you know what to do, you stay true. Fuck that snitch shit, you better than that. Kayne loves you, don't sell him out," she said softly. "I would serve life before I would ever give up my loyalty to Shawn. I know you might think it's easy for me to say that cause I ain't in your shoes, but that's real Mina. I love that nigga so much it hurts sometimes, and I know you love Kayne the same way." She looked me in the eye and I just nodded.

"Times up." The guard yelled looking in our direction.

"I'll write you." She threw her Louis Vuitton over her shoulder.

"Ok, I love you."

"I love you too, and I'm here now, remember that."

January 2, 2004

I woke up feeling good about my decision. I called my grandma as soon as I got my phone privileges. "Hi grandma." I tried to sound sincere when she picked up.

"Did you think about what I said?" She sounded annoyed.

"Yes. I thought a lot about it actually."

"Are you ready to use your head now?"

"Grandma, exactly what kind of information do they want?"

"They want to know about Kayne and his connect, where they met, how often they met and where they had crack houses at."

"Crack houses? What makes them think they had crack houses?"

"Well, not exactly crack houses but where they prepared their drugs, they'll ask if they ever stashed anything in you and Kayne's apartment?" She was starting to confuse me. I definitely wasn't fuckin' with it. I knew everything they wanted to know, but my lips were sealed shut. "This could bring your sentence down drastically. The police are desperate for this information."

"Yeah they are desperate, but for what? They already got him facing three years what else do they want, put him away for life? It just ain't that serious. You say this can bring my sentence down, but what will it do for Kayne? Put him deeper in the hole?"

"Kayne's already dug himself a damn ditch by not giving information. You don't have to be dumb, just because he is!" She was starting her tirade again, but it was my turn.

"I ain't being dumb and neither is he. He's followin' the code simple as that! I won't work against my man, I just won't do it. What am I rushin' home for anyway? My mama ain't no where to be found, and accordin' to you, my daddy don't give a fuck about me so ain't I just better off where I am?!" I was yelling now.

"Amina, you're grown. Make your own decisions. I wash my hands of this shit! If you ain't smart enough to save your own ass, I ain't gonna do it for you!"

"I won't save my ass by burning somebody else's!" I slammed the phone down, my decision was final. Three days later, I called Damen and told him the situation. He promised to talk to Savellman for me. He told me to give him two weeks to get in contact with him, I did. The next time I talked to him he said that I had to wait until Zelle got out and Savellman would work on my case. He also told me there was no garauntee he would be able to save me, but I kept my fingers crossed. For the next five months, Kayne and I wrote each other. I sent him a letter first, I wrote:

Dear Kayne,

Let me start by saying three words, I love you. I don't know if you know what's going on, so I'll tell you. The lawyer my grandma hired wants me to take a deal and give information about you and Wess. You know it ain't going down like that baby, so don't even worry about it. You know you can trust me. I don't care if they gave me life I wouldn't turn on you and you better know it. It was hard for me to tell my grandma no, but I did. I just don't think she understands how much I really love you. But I can't expect her to, 'cause it's something I can't even explain. I owe you my loyalty. All those nights you held me as I cried, told me my mom would be back, and that everything would be alright. Not once did you hurt me, Not once did you lay a finger on me when I would throw my little fits. You never even raised your voice, I'm not saying you should have, but I just want you to know that I appreciate the fact that you didn't. All those mornings I didn't feel like getting up for school, you

made me. If I didn't feel like driving, you drove me, just to get me to go. It's because of you that I made it as far as I did, and if it wasn't for me being dumb, I would have made it out. I blame myself for that completely. I ruined my life, not you. Just remember, as dumb as I may have been, I did it with you in mind. I just wanted to bring you home, and now I'll never see you again. I'm so sorry baby.

Love,

Amina

May 10, 2004

I got my most anticipated visit. He came in looking better than ever. Freshly dressed, iced out chain and wrist, fresh feet and 360 waves. He looked like he had never been in jail. He bounced back fast.

When he picked up the phone to talk, I didn't even look at him. I couldn't stand to. He had told me to be smart, and here I was in jail. I had been nothing but dumb.

"Look at me Amina." I looked up, but not in his eyes. "Look me in my eye," Zelle scolded me. I did it. At first there was silence, then he began. "I ain't gon say I told you so, because that won't help the situation. Really, I blame myself. If I had been out I could have protected you from all this. I'm sorry. I never thought things would end up like this, with me on the outside and you in."

"It ain't yo fault Zelle. I knew better, I just didn't wanna listen to anybody. I love Kayne so I wanted to do everything I could to get him out." He gave me a look I couldn't really read. I knew it was because I said I love Kayne. It must have shocked him. But there was no use in hiding anything now, everything was all out on the table.

"Derrick. He was the one that set you up that day?"

"Yeah. I should have known, but for some reason I trusted him."

"He was the one who took the cars. He sold 'em."

"What! How you know?"

"My nigga picked me up from jail in the Cadillac truck. He said he bought it from him for ten stacks."

"What about the CTS?"

"His brother bought it from Derrick for the same amount. I don't know who he sold the Yukon to."

"How did he get in there?"

"I don't know."

"Oh my God." I was in shock. I knew Derrick had set me up to take his fall, but I never thought in a million years that he was the one that had taken the cars.

"So, you ain't talked to Kayne?"

"Yeah, we write each other."

"Damen came to visit both of us when he was here. He cussed him out, I told him he can't blame Kayne. I know he didn't tell you to do what you did."

"No, I chose to. Was you in the same cell with him."

"Na, he was on a different floor but I saw him sometimes."

"I miss him so much. I don't wanna be in here. At least if I was out I could visit him."

"I know. You'll get out. I promise, it won't be 21 years, but-"

"Times up Moore," The guard interrupted, reminding me of the day I had visited Zelle in prison.

·

"I love you."

"I love you too." He got up to leave and the guard escorted me back to my cell. I couldn't get Kayne off of my mind. I found the very first letter he wrote me and re-read it like I did every night, it was my favorite one.

Amina,

You remember when I told you I loved you for the first time? Well I meant that shit. But now I love you even more. I'm not saying that I'm happy you locked down, cause that shit fuckin' me up.

After I got the visit from Damen in November, I damn near went crazy. I beat my inmate almost to death and spent the next three weeks in the hole. Every night, the thought of you sitting in a jail cell just like me, serving more time than me fucks with my head. Sometimes I think you too good to be true. The way you was so loyal to me, willing to do anything for me. I wish I never would have got that down chick shit in yo head, back when we was in Puerto Rico. Maybe shit wouldn't be so fucked up. But then when I think about it, you was down from the start because you just that real, and I love you more everyday for it.

Damen told me his biggest goal was to keep us apart. But he don't even have to try. These bars keep us apart. They keep me from yo beautiful face and perfect shape. They keep me from yo wet ass pussy that I wish I could hit from the back right now.

One day we gon be together again, and things gonna be like they used to. I'm gonna spoil you like I used to, you gonna have my seed. Shit gonna be perfect again. One day we gonna bounce back together.

Triple Crown Publications presents

Yo nigga,

Kayne

Chapter 23

"Come on Costello. You're out of here." The guard unlocked my cell, which I sat in alone. Slowly, I got up. It had been three long years; I was no longer the sweet 18-year-old. I was 21 and had lost so much in my life, and finally I was being given back my freedom. I walked to the front gate where I was being released. I was expecting to see Damen and Zelle, but standing there waiting for me was Kayne. I froze up, unable to move. I couldn't believe it. I had waited for this day for so long.

He walked over, kissed me and held me in this huge arms for a long time.

"I told you one day," he tilted my head up to look in my watery eyes. His face was the same but he looked older. His long cornrows were gone and he smelled so good. The last time I saw him he was still somewhat a boy but standing in front of me was a man, my man.

Finally I could shed tears of joy instead of tears of pain. I took advantage of the moment. The sky was bright and it was actually starting to snow. I inhaled the brisk air and felt alive. As I looked around I spotted a Porsche

"This us baby," Kayne said with a grin leading me to the car. Before he opened my door he went to the trunk and pulled out a Gucci bag. Inside was a long white Gucci leather. "It's cold out here, put this on."

"Where we goin?" I asked not really even caring. I was just grateful to be leaving prison. After three years anywhere sounded like paradise.

"Home. It's me and you now for real."

"How you pull this off?"

"Zelle convinced Savellman to get me out last year."

"Last year?" I didn't understand why he was just now showing up.

"So Savellman got me out too?"

"Yeah, he came through after I paid him off. I know it took me a long time. Zelle wanted me to get my shit together first. He didn't even want me visiting you. I don't blame him, he just want you to have the best. Shit gon' be different now. We legal now. Zelle got a barber shop over on Vine. Business is good, he's been there about a year. I just opened up a club last month." Kayne went on to tell me about all of the things that had happened since I got locked up. No one was hustling anymore, either they were dead, locked up or gone straight. After hearing those stories I was kind of glad I was where a was instead of out fighting in the streets.

We pulled into the parking lot of a new apartment building downtown. Kayne handed the valet the keys and took my hand, leading me to the entrance. .We rode the elevator to the sixth floor, and Kayne opened the door to a spacious loft apartment.

"Surprise!" A group of people shouted as soon as I stepped in. I wanted to run and change, put some makeup on and fix my hair. But it was too late, everyone had already seen me in my baggy jeans, sweatshirt and jailbird cornrows. When I looked around at everyone that was there, it didn't matter how I looked. There was Damen, Zelle, Shayna, Kelly, who had a baby in her arms standing next to her boyfriend Shawn, Trina, Brell, Swag, my grandma, my aunt Angie, and right in the middle of the crowd, holding a huge cake that matched the banner over the window that said "Welcome Home Amina," was my mother. She still looked as beautiful as I had remembered her. Tears streamed down both our faces as our eyes met. She sat the cake down and we hugged for what seemed like forever. I thanked everyone and said a little speech then greeted them all, one by one, with a hug.

It was hard to believe that after all these years, and all I had been through, I was back home with everyone I loved. After I showered and changed into a Prada dress that Shayna bought me, we all got stuffed on the food my grandma had prepared.

"I made this just for you Mi-Mi," she said hugging me again.

I sat down next to Kelly and Shawn at the breakfast bar in my new kitchen. She showed off her five-carat diamond engagement ring and introduced me to her seven-month-old daughter named Rayonna. She was so pretty, I held her for a while and then I went to talk to everybody else from the hood.

Swag was about to get signed by a big record company in New York. Brell had his own place in Avondale, and was working in Kayne's club located in Newport. Trina was in her third year at Florida State. She had flown in just for my homecoming. When I talked to my mom she told me everything that had happened with her and Markus. They had lived in Texas for a year. Finally, she left him and came home to live with my grandma until she bought a house in College Hill.

After getting over the initial shock of seeing everyone I was surprised by how beautiful my new home was. "I love it," I told Shayna who revealed that she had designed the whole thing for Kayne. She went on to tell me about how she and Damen got married. I wondered why no one had wrote to tell me about it. But it didn't matter now. I was home and that was all that mattered.

For some reason, Zelle couldn't take his eyes off of me the whole night. We really didn't get a chance to talk much but I know that he was just happy to see me smile again.

"It's time for presents!" Shayna shouted getting everyone's attention.

All the presents were mostly clothes and some cards with money. I was grateful for each gift. My mom gave me a locket with my name engraved on it, and a touching card that caused me to cry again. Damen handed me over the keys to a 2006 Mercedes Benz. I was back in style. Zelle gave me a Diamond charm bracelet with my initials, a heart, and a crown.

Then finally it was Kayne's turn. He handed me a small ring box, I opened it and was almost blinded by the eight-carat pink diamond ring.

"This ain't just a promise ring, I'm ready to make it official." He slid the ring on my finger and kissed me on the lips softly. I was speechless and so was everyone else around me. Silently, they waited for my response.

"Yes," I was finally able to whisper. Everyone went wild.

After everyone left, Kayne took me to his club. It was huge with three bars and two levels. No one was there but us so he turned down the lights, turned on a slow song, and opened a brand new bottle of Crystal. We sat in a VIP section. He pulled me close and whispered in my ear.

"Amina, you've made me the happiest man in the world."

"If you the happiest man then I must be the luckiest woman" I said, turning to kiss him. My mind flashed back through everything that had happened in four years. *This is how it's supposed to be. Me and him together with money to last and if I had to do it all over, I would still be down*, I thought.

I opened my eyes to find that I was still lying in my cell. It had all been a dream. Three years hadn't really passed, it was still May 10th 2004. I looked on the floor and saw a letter sitting there. The guard must have dropped it off while I was sleep.

Dear Amina,

I don't know how to tell you this, but I'll do my best. I called Terrance today and didn't get an answer. When I called his sister, she told me that he had been arrested for reducing her husband's years in jail. He's facing 45 years. Fortunately no one's found out about him helping Zelle out. Unfortunately, Zelle was the only one that made it out with his help. If I could, I would pay any amount to keep you from the next 21 years in jail. But I can't. Zelle is opening a barber shop downtown, so he'll be visiting often, and I promise to visit every chance I get. I love you so much. Your brother, and I promise we will never abandon you. Never. Stay strong.

Love,

Daddy

I ripped the letter into tiny pieces and let out a piercing scream, fell to the floor and started pounding my fists into the hard cold concrete. Four guards rushed to my cell. I continued screaming as they tried to force me under their control. I threw a complete fit. They dragged me to solitary confinement where I spent a whole night in tears.

When I finally drifted off to sleep I had another dream about Kayne. This dream picked up where it left off, and featured our wedding day. Of course it caused me to wake up screaming like a mad women again. I punched and kicked the walls, I pulled my hair and scratched my face. I was on suicide watch for two weeks. I was constantly hearing voices, so many of them. They were fucking with my head. The first voice I heard was my mother's, *"stop trying to mess up a good thing for me, I love him."* It echoed so loud I was sure the guards could hear her too. I tried to block her out. She repeated the same words over and over. I screamed and pulled at my hair. Just when I had begun to get rid of her voice, other ones came to haunt me. *"Bitch shut the fuck up!"* Tino shouted in my ear. I kicked and screamed, trying to escape the memory of him raping me. *"I'm sorry, I have to go back to Chicago, it's what's best for me,"* Damen whispered. "Daddy, don't leave me again..." I cried, curling up into a ball rocking myself back and forth. The voices only got worse. *"I'm gonna get his ass, just like I got Zelle."*

"Bitch! I'ma get you!" I screamed at someone who wasn't there.

Then I heard Shadow. *"Look, let's just do it a little easier. Let's just forget the poison and do stabbing instead."* My crying ceased, as I realized what I had done, I'd had somebody murdered. I began apologizing to no one in particular over a hundred times.

"I'm sorry...I'm so sorry..." I cried until Kayne's voice came to soothe me.

"Yeah, I love you, if I didn't I wouldn't be doing all this. It'll be three months on the 16th, and it's something different than it is with other females." I listened for more from him, *as I lay on the dirty mattress letting the wet tears dry on my face.* "What you know about hustlin' anyway? You crazy if you think I'ma have you out there like that. It ain't worth you riskin' yo life. I'll be aight."* I nodded in agreement as Kayne told me these words, this time. *"Go get you a place like I said. I gotta go, I love you. And stop cryin' this ain't the last you gon hear from me."* I wiped my tears. I believed him.

"Ok, I'll wait on you baby, I ain't goin' no where I promise when you get home, I'll be here." I failed to realize that it was too late.

The nurse came in and handed me a small plastic cup with two pills inside, and a cup of cold water.

"I'm feeling better, I don't need this." I told her handing it back to her.

"Yes, you do Amina. You've been doing good on taking your medication the last three days. Please don't give me trouble now." I stared at the pills.

"I talked to Kayne, he wants me to get myself a place to stay. He wants me to just wait on him. It's gonna be hard, but I can do it. Three years really ain't that long is it?" I looked at her for reassurance, she looked annoyed.

"Not really. Three years flies by. Take your pills Amina."

"Do they have any of those apartment magazines here? I need to find somewhere cheap right now, so I can pay for Kayne's lawyer."

"If you take the pills, I'll get you one."

"I don't want this damn medicine! What the hell I need medicine for? Get me one now!"

"Amina, I won't do it until you take your medication," she said calmly, standing directly in front of me with both hands on her hips.

"I ain't takin shit, I'm tired of being treated like some fuckin nutcase, I'm leaving!" I through the pills and the water on the other side of the room, and pushed her out of my way. She fell backwards onto the medication tray that she pushed in with her. I ran for the huge steel door, I kicked it and an alarm sounded I ran to the other side of the room. I already knew there was no other exit, but I searched for one anyway. I only found the same cement wall I'd been staring at for the last two weeks. Three guards and another nurse rushed in and straddled me to the floor. I couldn't kick or punch because the guards had me held down. The nurse bent down and shot me in the right arm with a needle filled with a clear liquid. I blacked out right away.

When I woke up, I found myself in a room with padded walls wearing a straight jacket I had been placed in a mental institution. I was kept there for three whole weeks because the voices kept coming, I was also having more dreams. It was like I was living my life through these dreams, they were all in order. Eventually they ceased, the voices stopped too. I was so relieved. When they did, I was transferred to a bedroom with a Spanish girl who loved to cut her wrist. She never said anything but I didn't care because neither did I.

207

Everyday at ten a.m., I attended a two-hour meeting with other girls my age. After that was lunch. I ate a turkey sandwich, plain Lays chips, an apple and a choice of milk or water every single day. After lunch I met with my private psychiatrist who reminded me so much of my mother. Believe it or not, I liked her. She encouraged me to use the dreams in a positive way. I agreed to try.

I begged her to get me in touch with Kayne so I could write him.

"I can't do that Amina. Writing him will do you no good. A simple letter is what got you here in the first place" she told me.

After that I began to hate her, just like I hated everyone else there. I shut everyone out, I didn't talk at the meetings and I refused to speak to my psychiatrist.

My punishment was no visitors until Christmas. That was seven whole months, but what did I care? Damen and Zelle didn't even know where I was. To my surprise though, they both showed up Christmas day but at different times.

Zelle gave me the exact same charm bracelet as he did in my dream. I started crying hysterically. He was then forced to leave, and I was sent to my room where I continued crying until Damen showed up that evening with the best Christmas present I could ask for—my mom.

"Baby, I'm so sorry." Was the first thing she said taking me into her arms.

Damen hugged me too, then we all sat down in the visitor room.

I told my mom everything, starting from the night I left home. When I finished, she was in tears right along with me.

"I'm so sorry. I never should have let you leave. I was so stupid," she said holding me again. An hour had passed and my visiting time was up. I went back to my room feeling better but still not willing to talk to anyone.

Three years have passed since Kayne and I were seperated, and sometimes I still have dreams and wake up in a fit. But after a while they just got tired of punishing me because it never helped.

Damen visits every major holiday, just like he promised. Shayna always comes along. My mom bought a house as close to the center as she could, and spends as much time with me as she can. My grandma visits too.

Zelle had a little boy named Canoray,. He brings him by every chance he gets but I've never seen the mother. I think they're separated.

A week ago, I overheard two nurses talking about someone not being able to visit me, because it would cause me to go into withdrawal again. They never said a name, only *"he."* When I saw Zelle yesterday, he told me they were talking about Kayne. Instead of crying or throwing a tantrum, I looked him in the eye calmly. "Just tell him that I love him, and if we ever got the chance to be together again, I would still be down." I meant every word of it.

ORDER FORM

Triple Crown Publications
2959 Stelzer Rd.
Columbus, Oh 43219

Name: _____

Address: _____

City/State: _____

Zip: _____

	TITLES	PRICES
	Dime Piece	$15.00
	Gangsta	$15.00
	Let That Be The Reason	$15.00
	A Hustler's Wife	$15.00
	The Game	$15.00
	Black	$15.00
	Dollar Bill	$15.00
	A Project Chick	$15.00
	Road Dawgz	$15.00
	Blinded	$15.00
	Diva	$15.00
	Sheisty	$15.00
	Grimey	$15.00
	Me & My Boyfriend	$15.00
	Larceny	$15.00
	Rage Times Fury	$15.00
	A Hood Legend	$15.00
	Flipside of The Game	$15.00
	Menage's Way	$15.00

SHIPPING/HANDLING (Via U.S. Media Mail)   **$3.95**

TOTAL $_____

FORMS OF ACCEPTED PAYMENTS:
Postage Stamps, Institutional Checks & Money Orders, all mail in orders take 5-7
Business days to be delivered.

ORDER FORM

Triple Crown Publications
2959 Stelzer Rd.
Columbus, Oh 43219

Name: _____

Address: _____

City/State: _____

Zip: _____

		TITLES	PRICES
		Still Sheisty	$15.00
		Chyna Black	$15.00
		Game Over	$15.00
		Cash Money	$15.00
		Crack Head	$15.00
		For the Strength of You	$15.00
		Down Chick	$15.00
		Dirty South	$15.00
		Cream	$15.00
		Hood Winked	$15.00
		Bitch	$15.00
		Stacy	$15.00
		Life Without Hope	$15.00

SHIPPING/HANDLING (Via U.S. Media Mail)   **$3.95**

TOTAL   **$_____**

FORMS OF ACCEPTED PAYMENTS:

Postage Stamps, Institutional Checks & Money Orders, all mail in orders take 5-7
Business days to be delivered.